Gary Russell

BBC BOOKS

THE "THANKS VERY MUCH" BIT

This book has been written speedily from an excellent script but with precious little visual reference. As well as that, changes to the script took place throughout filming and so portions of this version may differ from what we all see on screen.

Nevertheless, I am indebted to a number of people who have helped fill in the visual blanks, as it were.

To Rona and Nuala at BBC Books.
To Paul, Scott and, most importantly, Gary at Marvel UK.
To Kathy, who has always striven to keep me up to date.
To David, for patience above and beyond.

And especially to Jeff Bryer, Corey Klemow
and Bill Taylor:
I know none of the above three gentlemen, nor they me, but their postings on the InterNet have been invaluable.

Gary Russell
February 1996

DEDICATED TO

Terrance Dicks
*who made me want to write a
Doctor Who novelisation*

and to

Philip Segal
&
Matthew Jacobs

First published in the UK 1996 by BBC Books,
a division of BBC Worldwide Ltd, Woodlands,
80 Wood Lane, London W12 0TT
Text, design and layout copyright © BBC Books, 1996

Original series broadcast on the BBC
Format copyright © BBC 1963
Terry Nation is the creator of the Daleks.
Doctor Who, TARDIS and the Daleks are trademarks of the BBC

All rights reserved

ISBN 0 563 38000 4

Printed and bound in Great Britain by Clays Ltd, St Ives plc
Cover printed by Clays Ltd, St Ives plc
Colour separation by Radstock Reproductions Ltd, Midsomer Norton
Colour printed by Lawrence Allen Ltd, Weston-super-Mare

Out with the old . . .

The Doctor was lonely.

It had been a long time since he had last had the TARDIS to himself – in fact not since . . . well, surely since . . . no, it had been so long that he could not actually remember having been in the TARDIS alone. There had always been someone there with him; someone for him to educate, impart knowledge to, rescue from the fiendish clutches of some tentacled monstrosity or make tea for.

But recently he had spent far too much time tweaking and twisting various controls on the six-sided, mushroom-shaped console that dominated the six-walled main control room. He was always abstractly punching up destination after destination and, for the first time, finding none of them remotely attractive.

The whole universe, the whole of time and space to roam in, meddle gently in, right a few wrongs and enjoy some marvellous picnics, and yet he was bored.

For the sixth time in a month – at least it felt like a month, but time was relative, especially in a machine that was dimensionally transcendental – he had reconfigured the interior of the console room. He had moved away from its traditional bright white neo-futurism, with its high ceiling and roundelled walls, and gone for a much larger, more Gothic, redwood-panelled affair with walls stretching so far up that, at their apex, each one seemed to blend into the other.

Each wall reflected the basic instrumentation on the corresponding panel on the console. Opposite the data-bank switches for instance, the wall was row upon row of antique and modern books, forming the comprehensive TARDIS library.

The space/time destination panel faced a wall with every conceivable form of timepiece. Another panel, which ascertained how dangerous or safe the atmospheric conditions at any given location may be, was opposite a tiny secluded garden area, with an ornamental church organ borrowed from St Christopher's in Cheldon Bonniface, his favourite English village. Beside that was a stone fountain, a tiny fish pond full of rainbow gumblejacks, and a small stone bench, where the Doctor could sit and meditate whenever he felt the urge.

Another wall was a massive filing cabinet,

arranged alphabetically (although in eight hundred and forty three different languages) and full of the memorabilia collected after countless expeditions, adventures and investigations.

The Doctor still had not decided how to decorate the other walls, but he would in time. Probably.

Above the wooden main exit doors, with their marble embellishments, was a massive circular indentation, inscribed with the most recognisable Gallifreyan symbol: the Great Seal of Rassilon. Smaller versions of the device dotted the rest of this room and others. The Doctor had long resisted displaying them – he was not exactly proud of his heritage, but was now reaching an age (nearly one thousand years old) where it seemed to be appropriate to at least acknowledge it. He must be maturing, he decided, like a good wine.

His most recent upgrade had been to alter the appearance of the console. In place of high-tech touch-sensitive buttons were a series of gold-plated metallic switches, rods and cubes that had to be inserted into tiny slots, and countless dials providing the main control elements. The old scanner screen mounted into the wall had been replaced by one mounted on a flexible Z-spring that, every time he tugged on a rope, came out of the wall to wherever he was standing.

The floor of the console room and the rest of his TARDIS was now covered with the same redwood as the walls, an attractive parquet. Surrounding the small steps leading up to the console dais were wrought-iron arches, and a shiny brass railing topped off the now-enclosed console area.

This new look had a likeable touch of the eccentric about it. 'Very Gothic,' he had murmured after finishing the changes.

Now, however, the Doctor was already getting bored and he wondered if it was time to change it again.

He had just sat down with a cup of peppermint tea ready to read a book (a first edition hardcover of Herbert Wells's *The Time Machine,* inscribed personally to the Doctor by its author, who wrote that their time together had inspired much of it), when something odd happened.

He was distracted by a sound – more like a murmur – that rumbled through the TARDIS, as if from under the floor on which the Doctor stood. That was quite possible of course. The interior of the TARDIS, while not exactly infinite, was both vast and labyrinthian, with possibly hundreds of different rooms above and below the one he was in, let alone the ones to every side. A long corridor wound away from the console room, and frequently (and often at inopportune moments) the Doctor would dash through the door during some emergency, only to find that the TARDIS had reconfigured itself and he was lost. Of course, it might have been him who had reconfigured it – the more time he spent alone in his ship, the more frequently he forgot what he had done a few moments, days or even years ago.

It had been mentioned by more than one of the Doctor's travelling companions that the TARDIS itself seemed alive, or at least somehow capable of responding to the Doctor's moods and subconscious thoughts. More empathic than telepathic. The Doctor had never contradicted such theories. The truth of the TARDIS, his TARDIS especially, was his secret. And a man needed his secrets.

Then something even more extraordinary happened.

He heard a voice, calling. Not from inside the TARDIS but from inside his mind. A telepathic message, which could only have been sent by one of his own people.

It was very quiet, and he needed to concentrate to hear it clearly. Instinct more than anything else told him that this was not actually coming from his home planet – the message was too random and distracted. If it had been one of the Time Lords that dominated Gallifrey, from where he had fled so many years before, the message would have been crystal clear, extremely precise, cold, and boring. Rather like a majority of the Time Lords he had chosen to leave behind.

No, this was from another renegade like himself, and he immediately guessed who.

'The Master.'

The Doctor dropped on to the floor, sitting cross-legged, and closed his eyes, concentrating hard.

An image appeared in his mind's eye. It was indeed his oldest and most bitter rival, the Master, a fellow Time Lord who spent most of his lives plotting to destroy the Doctor and plunge the cosmos into chaos, his sole ambition being total dominance over all living things. Like all Time Lords, the Master could regenerate twelve times, giving him thirteen lives. Most Time Lords used those lives with wisdom and caution; each life capable of lasting a few thousand years before wearing out and needing to regenerate. The Doctor himself had gone through six previous bodies before his current one, but the Master had used his up a long time ago. Never one to let something as mundane as death cheat him of victory, however, the Master had found a variety of ways to prolong his life, usually involving adding alien genes to his own physical make-up. That way he had gone through at least one extra life recently.

It had once been suggested that the Doctor and the Master were opposite sides of the same coin; both Time Lords, both immensely powerful and intelligent. Whereas the Doctor was honest and good, compassionate and caring, the Master was the personification of total evil, malevolent and immoral.

Yet now the Master appeared to be in some sort of danger so fearsome that he was using his last reserves of mental energy to contact his greatest enemy.

The Doctor could see, projected into his mind, a dark room, with a central pillar of bright light in it. Standing erect, almost too erect, at the heart of it was indeed the Master, his saturnine features caught in a grimace of pain, clearly unable to move.

The Doctor caught a fleeting glimpse of a raised area totally surrounding the column of light, a group of metallic creatures looking down on the Master. He was clearly their prisoner.

A prisoner of the Doctor's other greatest foes, the Daleks; nasty mutated blobs of living matter existing inside metallic shells, all traces of conscience and morality purged from their existence. They lived to dominate and destroy. Like the Master, they were pure evil.

Unlike the Master, this time they seemed to have won.

The Doctor heard the familiar metallic grating voice of the creatures' leader, their Emperor.

'For your crimes against the Daleks, for your deliberate attempts to destroy us and usurp our rightful place as the supreme creatures of the universe, you are sentenced to extermination.'

The Emperor began listing the Master's crimes against the Daleks, citing various times they had joined forces, only for the Master to betray them at the last moment when it looked as if he was in danger of sacrificing his own being for their cause.

Many times before, the Doctor had thought the Master deserved all he got. Yet now, as he saw him immobile, and realised the extent of the Master's humiliation at having to contact the Doctor for help, he felt a great wave of pity for him.

They had grown up on Gallifrey together, been to the famous Academy together, and fled their regimented and boring lives for much the same reason, albeit with different intentions.

The Doctor's reverie was broken by the Master's voice echoing inside his mind again. The image of his foe, trapped in the harsh column of light, grew stronger.

'Doctor. Consider this my last will and testament. If I am to be executed and so cruelly deprived of all existence, I ask only that my remains be transported back to Gallifrey, my home planet, by you, my rival Time Lord and nemesis. Doctor . . .'

The Master's message was curtailed by a sudden chorus of 'Exterminate' from the assembled Daleks and the Master was hit from all angles by powerful energy weapons, his body contorting and twisting under the heat for a few seconds.

Possibly it was just the fading echo of the telepathic message being severed, possibly it was a result of the various chemicals and other artificial life-forces the Master had used to survive for so long, but instead of simply falling dead, his body glowed for a nanosecond and the Doctor could have sworn it turned almost crystalline before vanishing in a rush of light and heat.

The link cut off abruptly and the Doctor found himself now lying on his back, staring up at the dimly lit TARDIS ceiling, his head aching with the sudden termination of the telepathic connection.

Nevertheless, he knew that it was his duty to find a way of collecting the Master's remains from the Daleks' home world, and indeed returning them to Gallifrey.

All he would have to do, then, would be to get there undetected, sneak in unannounced, collect the Master's remains unobtrusively and leave again unnoticed.

Not an easy set of tasks but, as he'd once mentioned to some Ancient Greek or other, if you can't be bothered to clean the stables from top to bottom, don't bother picking up the brush.

Or something along those lines.

. . . in with the new

The Doctor struggled into the console room through the interior door which led to the corridor, half-dragging, half-carrying a massive wooden lectern. It had an eagle carved on top and a wide ledge on which once sat a Gutenberg bible. The lectern was almost as tall as the Doctor, but he managed to manhandle it to one side of the main TARDIS doors, next to a brass candelabra which held three everlasting candles. On the wide ledge of the lectern, he perched the casket that contained the Master's few remains.

Safely away from all other distractions, the Doctor took the opportunity to peek inside, feeling a twinge of both sadness at his one-time friend's fate, mingled with relief that the universe was at least safe from one of its most destructive characters.

The contents of the small, jewellery box-like casket were crystalline chunks. Only the Master's dark eyes still seemed recognisably intact. Even in death, the Master's hypnotic stare, now cast in crystal, was still disturbing. The Doctor closed the lid. He dug deep into his jacket pocket, and extracted a long, metallic, pen-shaped device with a circular top; a sonic screwdriver. Flicking a hidden switch on it, he aimed the device at the casket. A high-pitched whine emanated from the sonic screwdriver. A series of clasps on the box's lid snapped into place and a bolt slid home, shutting the casket. He adjusted the sonic screwdriver and the casket lid glowed momentarily, vacuum-sealing it.

'There.' He pocketed the sonic screwdriver. 'That should do it.'

With a last glance at the casket, the Doctor turned to the six-sided console, humming to himself as he flicked switches, twisted dials and punched buttons, setting a course for Gallifrey. He wondered briefly what reception his people would have for him. Sometimes, he was welcomed back with open arms, other times they tried to kill him. Still, it was these unpredictable moments that made life bearable, he supposed.

Behind him, the casket began to glow a dull green. Softly at first, but as time went on the glow got brighter. Then a crack appeared across the lid, followed by two more cracks, one down each side.

Finally, a small hole was bored through the lid from inside, sending a small set of silent green sparks into the air.

From this hole emerged something that was not quite liquid nor solid. An amorphous mass, it appeared almost snake-like due to the small hole it oozed through. The front end of it reared up slightly and two tiny eyes popped into existence, followed by a slitted mouth. It stared at the Doctor's back for a moment but then saw an opening on one of the TARDIS console's lower access panels, nearest the floor. Clearly the Doctor had been doing some adjustment or other and, in typical absent-mindedness, had forgotten to replace the panel securely.

It leaped soundlessly to the floor and darted towards the space, seeking the protection of the darkness.

The Doctor thought he saw a flash of movement out of the corner of his eye, but when he turned to look, there was nothing there.

Shrugging, he turned back to the controls, casting an eye to a tiny read-out screen on one panel. It read:

DESTINATION
Gallifrey
Constellation of Kasterborous
Local Dateline 5725.2

The screen flashed and went blank.
'Oh.' The Doctor waved away a small puff of

smoke and tapped the screen, but it remained resolutely blank.

He was about to ignore it, putting it down to the fact that the TARDIS was probably in need of a good overhaul, when three things happened at once.

First the time rotor, a cylindrical mechanism at the centre of the console, stopped its normally smooth in-flight rise-and-fall movement and shuddered slightly, as if moving was suddenly an enormous effort.

Second, from somewhere deep within the TARDIS, a low, rich bell tolled twice.

Third, another screen suddenly lit up:

CRITICAL TIMING MALFUNCTION
INSTIGATE AUTOMATIC
EMERGENCY LANDING

Then that screen went blank as well and cracked as a small explosion sent sparks towards the Doctor's face. The time rotor stopped completely and the TARDIS interior lights dimmed, bathing the Doctor in a burnt orange glow.

He shot a quick look to the base plates of the console and saw the damaged one, now lying free and flat on the floor. A dull green light throbbed from within the space.

The Doctor straightened up and hurried over to the cracked casket, taking in immediately what had happened. The Master had once again cheated death and had tricked him into bringing his 'remains' aboard his TARDIS. Whatever alien powers and abilities he had absorbed over the last few years had enabled him to survive the Daleks' execution. And whatever form his life essence currently inhabited was buried deep within the TARDIS systems and would need very careful expurgating.

Careful because the Doctor had no doubt that whatever else the Master was, he would by now be completely insane and unstable. The injuries that he had sustained had caused him to place whatever was left of his consciousness into a completely alien life-form.

And that made him more dangerous than ever before.

Chang Lee had been living dangerously ever since he was old enough to know how to pick up a gun. Ever since he had been about nine, in fact; just about eight years.

Back then, the Chang family had owned a prosperous corner shop, selling food and fancy goods to the San Franciscans in the Chinatown area. His father and mother had opened the shop from eight in the morning until nine at night, seven days a week, in an effort to keep them and their two sons Lee and Ho fed and clothed.

Then the triads had moved into their neigh-bourhood, bringing with them protection rackets and drug deals. Chang Ho, two years older than Chang Lee, had somehow got caught up in it all and before long was trying to persuade their father to sell crack under the counter at the shop, laun-dering money and generally acting as a distraction to the ever-vigilant Eighth Precinct.

Chang Lee's father had naturally refused, appalled by Chang Ho's behaviour. He would yell and shout that he had not devoted his entire life to the good of the community just to enable his son to become a petty criminal and ruin the family name. Chang Ho had replied that if his father failed to do what the triads wanted, well, Chang Ho was not responsible for what could follow.

Unperturbed by what he considered adolescent prattling, Chang Lee's father continued to run his shop the way he saw fit.

Until one day, on a warm April afternoon, when three members of a gang from the other end of Chinatown entered the store and demanded drugs. When Chang Lee's parents announced they did not deal, they were both shot dead. It was later claimed that this was a warning to everyone else in the area that the gangs and triads ruled Chinatown now.

By default, Chang Lee became part of the gang

Chang Ho ran with. The gang's aims were to make life as miserable for the locals as possible.

However, nothing lasted for ever and before long inter-gangland warfare broke out. Not just a few bar-room scuffles but major league stuff. One day Chang Lee was pick-pocketing tourists and such like, the next he was armed with a semi-automatic pistol, taking pot-shots at opposing gang members.

Chang Ho had died about three years back. A knife had slit his throat during some late-night break-in to a warehouse. Someone in their gang had set them up and the enemy gang was lying in wait. Alone now, Chang Lee had stuck around because it was the only way he knew to survive.

Life had been like that ever since; but now, Chang Lee decided, it might not carry on for much longer.

Not because he was able to get out or move to another state, but because here he was, three days off the millennium celebrations, running for his life down an alleyway linking Rose Street and Jasmine Boulevard. With him, equally terrified, were Pik Sim and Lin Wang, trying not to get shot in the back by the five men chasing them, firing their machine guns carelessly, not caring who got in the way.

Only three days before, Chang Lee had won the smart new black and orange baseball jacket and matching trainers from another gang member after a game of poker. If he had known he was going to be pelting through dark streets right now, he would have worn something less conspicuous. He must shine like a beacon to his pursuers!

Pik Sim suddenly pointed to her left, her long black hair wrapping around her face as she stopped.

'Down here,' she said urgently, pointing towards a tiny gap in the wall, leading somewhere.

'No,' said Chang Lee, 'no, it's a dead end.'

'No, it's not,' insisted Lin Wang, a couple of years older than Chang Lee. 'I've hidden down here before. We'll be safe.'

Chang Lee stared at them, panic-struck. 'You're both wrong, we can't –'

He stopped as a Crown Victoria swerved noisily into the other end of the alleyway, blocking their way forward. All three turned to face the way they had come, but at least four of the rival gang were hurrying down it, guns ready.

'Hide!' hissed Pik Sim, diving towards the small gap.

Chang Lee did not need to be told twice. He threw himself behind a row of trash cans, expertly avoiding making too much sound.

The car had stopped, its headlights catching Lin Wang in their beams. He raised his hands in surrender and was shot at least eight times, spinning around drunkenly before crashing against the opposite wall.

Foolishly Pik Sim ran towards him, screaming in fear and anger.

Chang Lee stared, horrified and unable to breathe as another volley of shots cut her dead before she even got near Lin Wang's body.

As she crashed to the ground, dead eyes staring forward in shock, Chang Lee heard an extraordinary sound. A peculiar wheezing and groaning seemed to come from all around, deep and strained.

Without thinking, Chang Lee stood up, staring. Beside the trash cans where he had tried to hide, a tall blue rectangular box simply appeared out of thin air, a light flashing on top. This was enough to expose Chang Lee's hiding place to the opposing gang and they opened fire. At first, the bullets went through the shape and Chang Lee ducked down again, avoiding them. As the box solidified, the bullets began bouncing off it and seconds later the light stopped flashing.

If that was not enough of a surprise for Chang Lee, he got a bigger one when a door of the box opened inwards and a small westerner in a straw hat walked calmly out, grinning. He was wearing checkerboard pants and a tweed sports jacket, leather patches on the elbows, over what seemed to be an expensive white silk shirt and complementary felt tie. He was examining a gold fob-watch – probably worth a fortune – hanging from the pocket of his burgundy vest. In his other hand he swung a red-handled umbrella. His peculiar and sudden materialisation did not seem to have fazed him; he carried a look of someone who did strange things every day.

The strange man had barely moved two steps before a second wave of bullets meant for Chang Lee smashed into him, hurling him back against the box. Eyes staring wildly in pain, he grabbed at a tiny handle on the door, pulling it closed before slumping to the ground, shaking violently.

Chang Lee heard the startled cries of his would-be assassins and saw them rush down the alley, past him and the dead man, and jump into the car which reversed backwards and away with a screeching of tyre rubber on Tarmac.

Seconds later, all Chang Lee could hear was a dog, disturbed by the gunfire, barking madly and a faint police siren. He crossed to the man and was astonished to find him still breathing, although he was bleeding badly from the bullet wounds. Chang Lee glanced across at Pik Sim and Lin Wang. They were certainly dead and there was nothing he could do, but this man had inadvertently saved him, at a terrible cost. Normally Chang Lee would have just accepted death as something that hap-pened around Rose Street, but there was some-

24

thing about this man and his amazing blue box that made him wait.

'Timing malfunction . . .' The little man was trying to speak; his accent sounded British – Irish or something, perhaps? 'Shouldn't be here . . .' Then the man gripped Chang Lee's arm. 'Look! Don't let it . . . escape . . .' He was pointing backwards, towards the door. Chang Lee could not see what the little man was talking about, but felt him become a dead weight.

'Too late. He morphed out. Through the TARDIS lock.' He shook Chang Lee's wrist. 'Stop it. You have to stop it.'

'Stop what?' Chang Lee did not understand any of this. What was there to stop? 'Hold on there, old guy. Chang Lee will find a way to help you.'

A police car suddenly swerved into the alley-way and two police officers jumped out, guns up and aimed at Chang Lee.

The amorphous snake-creature that housed the Master's consciousness reared up, like a cobra ready to strike. It was watching the whole scenario from beside the trash cans, hidden in the shadows. The Doctor had seen it escape the TARDIS, but the boy had not. It stared at the youngster, but decided the body was not mature enough for what it needed. It knew it could not remain in this state for long. If the Master was to live again, he needed a new body. Preferably a Time Lord body, which is why it had needed to be within striking distance of the Doctor in the first place. It had to place the life within it into a reasonably Time Lord-like body before too long or it would dissipate.

With the Doctor out of reach, a human would have to do for now.

An ambulance pulled up at the end of the alley-way and within moments, the strange little man's body was on a stretcher, being carried to the warm haven of the vehicle. A drip was set up and inserted into the patient's arm and another machine monitored his extremely slow heartbeat.

One paramedic drove, the other settled in the back with his patient. One of the police officers walked over.

'Better take this one with you. He's called Chang Lee apparently and he's not carrying. He seems concerned about your patient.'

The paramedic looked at the Chinese boy and then helped him into the ambulance.

'Will he be all right? Is he going to live?'

The paramedic shrugged, and gripped his seat as the ambulance started up its siren, rushing back towards the nearest hospital with ER facilities. He reached across his patient, ripping away the blood-stained shirt.

'What a mess.' He looked at Chang Lee. 'You know this guy?'

'Yeah,' lied Chang Lee. 'Yeah, we were just passing when –'

The paramedic ignored him. 'Yeah, right. Is he rich?'

Chang Lee shrugged.

The paramedic continued swabbing at the injured man's shoulder with a rapidly reddening antiseptic swab. 'Well, he'd better be rich, because where we're going, he'll need some cash.'

He reached to a pocket attached to the opposite wall, taking out a sheaf of papers.

'Here, sign these for him,' he said, passing them to Chang Lee.

'I don't sign anything, Mr –'

'Gerhardt. I'm Bruce Gerhardt. And it's just a release form. Sign it or he'll end up dying.'

Chang Lee took the proffered pen, scribbling a few lines on the form. 'What's the date, Bruce?'

'December 30th . . .' replied the paramedic.

'1999,' Chang Lee finished. He handed the paper back.

Bruce looked at it, then back at the man. 'Well, Mr Smith . . .' He sent a look straight at Chang Lee, suggesting that he did not believe the man's name was really John Smith at all. 'Your friend here hopes you'll be all right. So do I, so just lie back and we'll take care of you.'

Chang Lee found himself hoping that Bruce was right and the man whose name he'd just decided was John Smith (and he had no idea why he chose that name) really would be all right.

After all, if he was rich, there was bound to be some kind of reward.

At the side of the alleyway, the amorphous shape of the luminous snake had tried to edge forward. Its skin was beginning to crystallise; it needed to find something organic. Something it could get inside and meld with. Something to survive within, before the mental energy – the life-force – contained within it withered and died. The hardening of its mucous body meant that it had to do something quickly.

In using all its energy to form eyes with which to transmit information to the Master's mind and a mouth through which it could take in oxygen and other chemicals it needed to survive, it had little energy left. No way to create vocal chords to call for aid, or any form of weaponry. All it possessed was enough energy to get nearer the Doctor and find a way to get inside his body. Once there, the Master would do the rest.

It had dragged itself towards the open door of the ambulance and hurled itself in. It landed under the empty front passenger seat, unseen by the driver who slammed all the doors shut and drove on.

Walker General Hospital, San Francisco, was preparing itself for a busy few days. With the millennium celebrations approaching in less than forty-eight hours, all staff were on overtime, anticipating a greater number of accident and emergency cases than most New Year's Eves in the past.

Its ER department was unusually quiet during the early evening of December 30th, so when the ambulance screeched to a halt outside reception, the staff inside were almost relieved to have something to do.

As Bruce flung open the back doors, Chang Lee was gratified to see two nurses and what appeared to be a young doctor ready to help place the man who had saved his life on to a stretcher and rush back towards the reception area.

Bruce and Chang Lee hurried after them, the paramedic shouting that the patient had three gunshot wounds, adding almost as an afterthought that his heart had begun to go wild as well. 'Probably on something,' Bruce muttered to Chang Lee.

Chang Lee looked around the brightly lit reception, catching the eye of a pretty red-headed receptionist.

'You with the trauma case, sir?'

Chang Lee nodded.

'You sit right down there.' She pointed at a row

of moulded red plastic seats. 'I'll let them know you're here, but it might be some time before you hear anything. You want a coffee, there's a machine down there.' She jabbed her pen towards a corridor opposite where they had taken the Doctor. 'Toilets are there as well.'

Bruce flicked through his sheets of paper and then passed them to the red-headed receptionist. 'Pass these on, will you?'

The receptionist nodded. 'See you in the New Year, Bruce.'

'Yeah,' he replied, walking back towards the doors. 'Have a good one.' He glanced at Chang Lee. 'See you, kid.'

'Thanks, Bruce,' said Chang Lee, fidgeting nervously. He'd never been to a big hospital like Walker General before. Most injuries he'd seen were treated by a couple of back-street medics who took payment in little plastic bags rather than cash. He watched through the glass doors as Bruce climbed back beside the driver of the ambulance and it drove away. Then, he settled down to wait and see whether the strange man died.

Jim Salinger was the resident on duty, and it was his job to make initial recommendations and judgements on ER cases. Beside him, Shelly Curtis and Angela Wheeler, the two duty nurses, stared in surprise at the X-ray hanging in front of them.

Beside them, on the stretcher under a massive X-ray machine, was the patient. His clothes cut from the top half of his body and the wounds cleaned, he lay still, just breathing heavily and erratically.

Curtis ran her pen top gently around the image that caused so much consternation. She scratched her head with the same pen, absently. 'Two hearts,' was all she could say.

Salinger could not really argue, so he just shrugged. 'I've not seen anything like it.'

Wheeler was busying herself with further details of their patient's injuries. 'One bullet went straight through his shoulder, causing no life-threatening damage,' she reported. 'The other two are in his left leg and –'

She broke off as her associate's words sunk in. 'Two hearts?'

Salinger was shaking his head. 'No, it can't be. Must be a double-exposure.'

He tugged the X-ray down off the light-box. 'C'mon, people. Let's get those bullets out of him.'

They wheeled him through a set of double doors and into the main area of the Trauma Room. Curtis watched as Wheeler, the more experienced of the two nurses, helped Salinger remove the bullets. Moments later, it was done and the tiny silver tray Wheeler carried contained three blood-stained rounds of ammunition.

Curtis pointed at the read-out on the ECG. 'His heart is still going like crazy,' she said.

Salinger glanced up. 'Okay. We'd better get cardiology in.'

Curtis nodded, crossing to a telephone by the door. 'Yeah, okay. Whose turn is it tonight?'

Salinger smiled. 'Grace Kelly . . .'

The Grand Metropolitan Opera House was one of San Francisco's most glamorous hot-spots; the sort of place that people who had been out of the public eye for too long – but not according to their publicists – went to be seen by the society hostesses and paparazzi.

The Opera House had been built just one year earlier to commemorate the forthcoming millennium. Like its sister building in London, it was specifically constructed so that it could be dismantled and reassembled anywhere else if need be.

Despite those modern trappings, the interior was designed with a sort of retro-Twenties art-deco feel, featuring a number of abstract carvings and walls lined with famous opera stars of the past caught in silhouette, only their lips or fingernails picked out in reds or yellows.

The opera selected to see in the twenty-first century was an early twentieth-century one – Puccini's *Madame Butterfly*. A story about a nineteenth-century American serviceman whose less-than–saintly behaviour ultimately leads to the suicide of his young geisha wife.

Watching that evening's performance, dressed to kill, were a couple in their early thirties. They looked slightly out of place in a row of elderly patrons of opera who had noisily got tired of listening to the young woman summing up the plot for her clearly ignorant young partner.

Butterfly was currently singing *Un bel dì Vedremo* to her maid, Suzuki. The man asked exactly what was going on, for what must have been the tenth time.

'She's convinced that Pinkerton is going to come back one day.'

'She's stupid. He isn't, we all know that.'

'Yes,' said the woman through gritted teeth, 'but *she* doesn't. She's a naive teenager in Japan who thinks the Great White Man is honourable.'

The ageing couple to her right tutted, meaningfully.

The woman smiled at them. 'Sorry, Brian seems to have missed a bit.'

'Probably because you were telling him about an earlier bit, then,' grumbled the old man.

The younger woman sighed. 'Yes. I'm really sorry. It won't –'

A pager went off in her handbag.

This time, everybody sighed and casting a look of apology at Brian, she stood up and stumbled out of her seat, knocking into people's knees and apologising every other step.

She walked slowly up the stalls stairs, emerging into the box office area, blinking in the sudden bright light.

The bleeper went off once again, and one of the smartly dressed ushers pointed her towards a public phone before she even had to ask.

It was easy to see why her colleagues referred to her as Grace Kelly – she resembled the famous glamorous actress in more than just her luscious cascade of strawberry blonde hair. Her figure, accentuated by the tight electric-blue ballgown she was wearing, was the sort that most modern actresses would have had to pay a small fortune to have implanted, and her face might well have been carved from a marble statue of a Greek goddess. Although not in any way harsh, she had a defined bone structure along with a generous mouth and piercing blue eyes which appeared to be laughing no matter how serious she was being.

She punched in a call-collect number and seconds later it was answered.

'It's Grace Holloway. What's the problem?'

There was a brief explanation and she acknowledged it. 'I'll be there in ten.'

She replaced the receiver and walked back to the usher. 'Where can I get a cab from?'

He pressed a button on the wall beside him and

through the main entrance, Grace could see a yellow bulb light up. Ten seconds later a taxi pulled up and she thanked the usher, dashed outside and got in the cab.

'Walker General, please. ER reception.'

The cab driver nodded and drove quickly away.

Ten minutes later, Grace was in her pastel blue work gown, a surgical mask suspended below her chin.

'. . . and fibrillation at three hundred,' Jim Salinger was saying.

'No blockages showing?'

Salinger shook his head. 'No, Dr Holloway.'

'X-rays?'

'NG.'

Grace raised her eyebrows. 'No good? Why not?'

Salinger shrugged. 'Double exposed. Every time we tried one.'

'Well,' Grace snapped on a pair of surgical gloves, 'try again, Jim.'

Salinger nodded. 'Curtis is setting a new machine up right now. But it'll take at least half an hour.'

Grace shoved her hair under a white surgical cap with experienced ease. 'No time for that then. Come on, we'd better get moving.'

The double doors from the operating theatre

opened and Shelly Curtis hurried in, a mobile phone in her hand.

'Dr Holloway, it's Brian.' She held the phone out as if it might bite her.

Grace, used to Brian's short fuse where her work was concerned, knew how she felt. 'Yeah, well, I'm sorry, but he knew I was on call before we went out tonight.' She stared at Curtis, who just passed her the phone. 'What was I supposed to do, Shelly? Ignore it?'

Curtis gave her an 'I've heard this one before' look and walked away, leaving Grace to talk into the phone. With a sigh, Grace said hello to Brian.

There was a tirade from the other end, Salinger presumed, watching and waiting to see the outcome.

'I'm sorry, Brian, but I had to go . . . Oh, come on, don't say that, I . . . No, wait until I get back, please and we'll talk about it.' Grace shot a look of helplessness to Salinger and he just smiled at her, rather unhelpfully. Grace spoke again. 'No, don't be silly, just – Brian? Brian?'

Salinger watched as Grace lowered the phone, switched it off and crossed the room to drop it on to a chair.

'Gee, I'm sorry,' he said, not being sorry at all.

Grace picked up her handbag, taking out a cassette tape. 'Music while we work, all right, Jim?'

He nodded. 'No problems. You're the Doc.'

Grace put on her protective mask and they crossed through the double doors and into the operating theatre.

Just outside the theatre area, Dr Roger Swift was taking a group of smartly dressed men and women for a late night stroll through the hospital. As Walker General's administrator, it had been the businesslike Swift's job to represent the hospital at a fund-raising event in one of San Francisco's more popular (and expensive) restaurants.

Having talked himself hoarse trying to keep current and potential investors interested in the hospital, Swift had been dismayed when the eccentric, widowed and rather rich Mrs Carrington lifted a bejewelled hand and asked for a guided tour.

'I'm not sure I can arrange that right now, Mrs Carrington,' Swift had mumbled.

'Oh, nonsense, dear boy,' the old witch had replied, 'of course you can. Go and phone someone up to let us in, and,' she sniggered at the guests fawning around her, 'be swift about it.'

With the 'polite' laughter of the group – which reminded him of a pack of hyenas – ringing in his ears, Swift had contacted the security people, listing everyone's names so that there would be no embarrassing moments when they arrived at the hospital.

He ordered a fleet of cabs to take everyone there, ensuring that the cabs would wait and then take everyone off to wherever they wanted to go.

'Cost more to do this than I'm asking them to put up,' he grumbled to himself as he visited the men's room on his way back to the table.

By the time he was with his group, his fixed smile had returned and he announced to Mrs Carrington and her hangers-on that their carriages awaited to escort them to San Francisco's finest medical facility.

Now here they were, in the warm confines of Walker General. Swift was proudly showing them whatever latest pieces of machinery or equipment he could find, describing them in educated detail, safe in the knowledge that no one had the slightest clue what he was talking about. Blind 'em with science and hopefully they'd cough up the readies and go away, leaving him to get on with his job.

'And here,' he said, waving an expensively-manicured hand towards a door, 'here is the observation gallery for the Electro-physiology theatre.' He quickly looked inside, peering through the glass partition on the opposite side and into the lab. 'If we're very careful,' he said, trying to make out he was letting them in on something top secret, 'we can go in and watch. Dr Holloway is operating now.'

He led them in and grouped them by the

partition, ensuring that Mrs Carrington had the best view. He pointed into the theatre, and said quietly to Mrs Carrington, 'That's Dr Grace Holloway, one of our senior cardiologists.'

'She's a bit young, isn't she?' Mrs Carrington croaked back.

'Dr Holloway may look young to us,' he stressed, hoping that Mrs Carrington would feel he was bringing her down to his age rather than elevating himself into senility, 'but I can assure you, she is the best in her field. Quite the expert which we pride ourselves on having here at Walker General.'

He pointed at something in her hands. 'Dr Holloway will now insert a microsurgical probe into the patient's artery, then search out the short-circuiting part that is causing the fibrillation. And,' he smiled benignly at them all, 'just so that you can see how your money is being well-spent, she'll blast it with lasers.'

A few moments before she noticed Roger Swift bringing what appeared to be a senior citizens' coach party into the observation gallery, Grace Holloway had been talking to her patient.

It had been just after she had slipped her tape into the battered beat-box in the corner – she liked to have music on while she worked. Unorthodox, but it helped her concentrate.

39

'If I can't see it live, I'll hear it on tape,' she had said to Angela Wheeler, as the second half of Act Two of *Madame Butterfly* began anew. Wheeler passed Grace the microsurgical probe she would be using.

Appropriately enough, the lullaby Butterfly sings to her baby son Sorrow, *Dormi amor mio,* began as Grace stared at her comatose patient.

And his eyes had snapped open, staring straight into her face.

She took a slight step back, but then smiled at him. 'Hello. You're quite safe.'

'Puccini,' he said quietly. 'It's *Madame Butterfly.*'

He suddenly turned his head from side to side, presumably taking in where he was. 'Whatever you're about to do,' he had rasped, 'please don't.' His head fell back, eyes closed. 'Just stop.'

Grace had looked over at Salinger and Wheeler. 'Note: going by his strong accent, the patient is from Scotland. Probably a tourist. He might not be covered by insurance.'

Salinger had shrugged. 'Okay, what do you want to do?'

'Go ahead, anyway. Something is damaging his heart and we haven't got time to mess about with all that paperwork.'

She looked back at the man, as Curtis dabbed his head with a damp cloth. 'Mr Smith? You're going to be okay.'

He had looked up at her again. 'No, you don't understand.' His breathing was clearly hurting him now. 'I'm not the same as you. I'm not even human –'

Grace smiled. 'Well, no one's the same as me, Mr Smith.'

He then reached up and gently held her wrist, as if to stop the microsurgical probe going near him. 'I don't need that. I need a beryllium atomic clock!'

Grace had looked across at the other three. Salinger tapped his head, indicating that he thought the patient was crazy. Wheeler nodded her agreement. Curtis just dabbed his forehead again.

Beside them, the ECG machine's beeping was getting louder.

The patient had become insistent, his blood pressure rising. 'Tell me,' he begged. 'This is 1999, isn't it?'

Salinger was frowning at the ECG. 'We can't wait any longer, Grace.'

Grace had nodded and Salinger picked up the oxygen mask, sliding it down the patient's face.

The patient's next, muted, grunt had been something else about him not being human, but again Grace just put that down to the trauma of his injuries.

'Don't try to speak now, Mr Smith,' she said.

'We've removed the bullets, but we still need to know what's making your heart go wild – so that I can fix it.'

The patient had begun struggling, weakly.

'Now don't worry,' Grace tried to reassure him, 'I've done hundreds of these.' She indicated for Salinger to inject the patient with anaesthetic.

Grace had leaned forward to see if her patient had gone under, when he suddenly sat bolt upright, eyes wide, staring straight at her.

Piercing blue eyes that seemed suddenly very clear, very determined, very powerful. He grasped her wrist again, this time as if to warn her. He was clearly very serious but also very frightened of something. And for a brief moment, Grace had the feeling that he was rarely afraid of anything.

'Timing malfunction. The Master! He's out there,' he said. 'I've got to stop him.' And then his eyes rolled back, closed and he slumped unconscious on the table.

Grace prised her wrist out of his grip, shaking slightly. There had been something about the utter conviction with which he had spoken, the fierce honesty in his eyes.

If only it had made some kind of sense.

As she cleared her head, thinking about the microsurgery, she glanced over at Shelly Curtis. 'Somehow, I don't think his real name is John Smith at all, do you?'

Roger Swift had then interrupted her reverie by bringing his visitors into the observation gallery and so she had begun work, probing, watching the results on the screen suspended just above her patient.

'So, is Brian threatening to leave again?' asked Salinger.

Grace grunted. 'He won't.'

'Look, Grace, this is becoming a habit.' Salinger leaned across at her. 'If you want a replacement, I am house-trained.'

Grace was not sure exactly how serious Salinger was. She just smiled at him. 'Yeah, right. Forget it, Jim.'

Sarcastically, Jim smiled. 'Why, thank you ma'am.'

Grace did not respond. Instead, she frowned and then clicked her fingers towards the beat-box.

Wheeler flicked it off.

'This is strange . . .' Grace frowned.

'What?' asked Salinger.

'Déjà vu.' Grace moved the probe very slightly. Without looking up, she indicated the screen with her head. 'Where am I?'

'Sub-clavian.'

'But I should be in the brachiocephalic.'

Salinger laughed. 'Not unless he's a donkey.'

Curtis and Wheeler laughed, probably more than anything else to try and break the sudden tension Grace could feel in the air. She, however, was deadly serious. 'Let me try something,' she muttered, stabbing the red button nearest her.

The patient's body, Smith or whoever he really was, reacted violently.

'Massive seizure,' yelled Salinger, darting around the ECG machine, making adjustments. 'Grace, get the probe out of there!'

'I'm trying!' Grace could not understand what had happened. It was as if the body was rejecting the probe, literally trying to fight it. 'I am trying.'

'Picture's out,' announced Curtis, attempting to reactivate the monitor.

Simultaneously, Wheeler was checking the patient's vital signs. 'We're dropping off fast. We're losing him.'

Salinger looked almost ready to thump the ECG machine in frustration. 'Just get it out, Grace. Pull it.'

Grace felt she was almost coaxing something living, as if the probe had become part of the patient's body. 'Come to me,' she said softly. 'Come to mamma.'

Suddenly there was an elongated beep, no rhythm, no pulsation.

'Grace,' said Salinger, his voice quiet. 'Grace, he's flat lining.'

Grace barely heard him. She was staring at her empty hand and the tiny keyhole wound in the patient's chest where the probe had been. 'I got lost in there . . .' was all she could say.

Salinger suddenly pushed her back. 'He's going, Grace!' In his hands, Salinger had the paddles, linked up and ready. 'Stand back.'

Grace, feeling disorientated and bemused, stepped back, letting Salinger attempt to revive their patient. She glanced over to the observation gallery, where Swift was slowly ushering his friends away.

As Swift left, he stared back at Grace. The message in his look was unmistakable. An error had been made, a patient had died in Grace's care during a routine operation and Swift saw it as her responsibility.

So did she.

She stared at the ECG monitor, mentally begging for a response.

'Give me three hundred,' Salinger said to Curtis, and then shouted 'Clear' to everyone. They moved back and he attempted a further resuscitation.

Grace lost count of the subsequent attempts – all she could do was remember the man's face. And his astonishingly fierce eyes. Full of strength. Full of pain. Full of fear.

Eventually she became aware of Salinger talking to Wheeler and Curtis.

'Time of death?'

'Twenty-two oh three.' Curtis countersigned the report. She turned to look at Grace. 'I'm sorry, Dr Holloway.' She left, followed by Wheeler.

Salinger was looking at her. 'Need your signature, too.' He held out the clipboard and she took it, signed and passed it back in one fluid movement, as if she did it every day.

No one that she could remember had ever just given up and died like that.

No one should have to. She looked into Salinger's eyes, trying not to cry. 'Jim. I got lost. I just don't understand . . .'

'Grace,' Salinger shrugged. 'It happens.'

She stepped back. 'No, Jim. Not to me. I want another look at those X-rays.'

Salinger nodded.

'Now,' she barked.

As Salinger went to find them, Grace yanked off her surgical gloves and cap and threw them to the floor. After staring at them for a moment she went back into the prep room, gathered her opera gown, shoes and bag and headed out to her office, passing a couple of cleaners and a rather overweight young porter who looked as if he lived on a diet of burgers and cola.

She stopped. 'Pete?'

The porter, in his regulation blue smock and white boots, smiled.

'Hi, Doc. What can I do for you?'

She pointed back to the theatre. 'Morgue.'

Pete grabbed a bleeper from his breast pocket. 'Sorry, Doc. Don't take it too hard.' He punched up a number on his bleeper. 'Ted'll bring up the trolley.'

'Thanks, Pete. Store him.'

Pete acknowledged her order and headed for the theatre.

What could have gone wrong? Why was she so convinced there was something strange about this mysterious Mr John Smith?

She entered her office to find Angela Wheeler rummaging through a bag with the patient's belongings in them. A sling, a browning apple core, a cricket ball, a long, silver thing that might have been a torch . . . a variety of useless objects.

Wheeler just shrugged. 'No identification at all, Doctor. I'm sorry.' She replaced them in the bag.

Pete put his head round the door. 'Doc? Mr Salinger asked me to give you these.'

'Thanks, Pete.' Grace took an envelope from him and he left.

They were the X-rays, and so Grace placed them on her light-box. She stared at them for a moment, and Wheeler joined her.

'What shall I do, Doctor?'

Grace continued looking at the two hearts, so clearly there. 'Tag him as a John Doe and book him for an autopsy.'

Wheeler turned to go. 'D'you want me to get that Chinese kid that came with him in? Maybe he can give us an ID?'

Grace just stared at the X-ray. The answer was there. It had to be . . .

'Dr Holloway? The kid?'

Grace closed her eyes, needing to break her own concentration. 'Yeah, the kid. Sure.'

Wheeler went out and Grace looked back at the X-ray. 'No, Jim. This is not a double-exposure at all.'

There was a knock on the door and she turned to see Wheeler escort a Chinese youth in.

'Thanks Angela. I'll see you tomorrow.'

'Sure. 'Night, Dr Holloway.'

Grace went and sat behind her desk as the kid watched Wheeler go.

'She's nice,' he muttered.

'Yeah,' said Grace. 'And she's married. And you're too young for her.'

She picked up a pen and waved him to a seat on the opposite side of her desk, by the bag. 'Now, I'm Dr Holloway. And you are?'

'Chang Lee.'

'Okay Chang Lee. You a friend of Mr Smith?'

Chang Lee looked at the pen rather than Grace. 'Yeah. Sort of. Is he okay?'

Grace stared at the boy. He was only about sixteen, maybe seventeen. And clearly bewildered.

'Look, there were complications.' Talk about understatements. 'I'm afraid he didn't make it.' She saw Chang Lee's jaw clench slightly, then he relaxed.

'It's okay.' Chang Lee was staring intently at the bag of possessions. 'I'll tell his family.' He reached out to the bag. 'These his things?' He opened the bag, frowning as if he didn't recognise any of the contents.

Grace took the bag and moved it to her side of the desk. 'I think we at Walker General ought to contact his family ourselves.'

Chang Lee shook his head vehemently. 'No, Doctor. No, this'll hit 'em hard. I'll tell them –'

Grace stood up, and Chang Lee shifted back in his seat, ignoring the bag. 'I don't think you knew this man at all. Did you?'

Chang Lee tried to look indignant. 'Yes I did!'

'Fine. Then tell me his real name.'

Chang Lee stood up as well. 'I gotta go, man.'

Grace folded her arms. And Chang Lee seized the chance he clearly been waiting for. His hand darted forward, scooped up the bag and he dashed out of her office.

'Wait,' Grace yelled, following him. By the time she was in the corridor, he was at the far end, heading for reception. She set off after him.

She reached reception, only to see Chang Lee nearing the exit. Grace shouted at the red-headed

49

receptionist to try and stop him, but she just looked rather bewildered. Chang Lee was gone.

'Damn.' Nothing had gone right this evening.

Some time later, Pete and Ted were wheeling Grace's mysterious dead patient towards the body room section of the morgue. They pushed it through the double doors and stopped inside a room full of metallic rectangular doors, each one leading to a cold room where bodies could be stored on their gurneys.

Ted picked up a sheaf of papers. 'Number Eight is empty.'

Pete nodded, and wandered over to Number Eight, opening the door. 'You doing anything for New Year's Eve, Ted?'

The body, now stripped of all its clothes, was wrapped in a grey shroud which Ted was tying up at the back. 'Same as you, I guess. The upstairs fancy dress party. Going as Wild Bill Hickok.'

Pete was not sure who Wild Bill Hickok was – he was sure he knew most actors and pop stars – so he just smiled. 'Great.' He picked up a name tag and scribbled *JOHN DOE* on it before wandering back towards the body. 'Taking Barbara with me. Should be fun.'

He attached the label to the dead man's right big toe. 'John Doe on the toe,' he said to the dead body. 'We got a nice autopsy booked for you. First thing in the morning, mister. Then that's followed by a sauna or a Swedish herbal wrap. What would be your pleasure?'

Shrugging at the lack of response, he glanced over at the huge clock by the door. 'Hey, Ted, it's one in the morning. It's New Year's Eve, 1999. Party on . . .'

Ted rolled the body off the trolley and on to Number Eight's gurney. He then slid it back inside and locked the door.

'Yeah, let's rock, Pete.'

Inside Number Eight, something very strange was happening.

Normally, a dead body would lie there until its autopsy, untouched and unmoved.

This mysterious body, however, began quivering. A strange glow lit up the shroud and for a moment it seemed to melt away, revealing a starscape; suns, moons and planets, swirling gas giants and flaming comets. As if the whole universe was encased within the outline of one man's body.

Then it all faded back to normal, and the body was lying inside its grey shroud.

Normal until the man's hand moved from inside the shroud and ripped it away. For a moment, the revealed body just lay there. Then the eyes popped open. Bright eyes, shining with life.

Life that did not want to be shut inside whatever dark prison it had been incarcerated. But it was tired. Exhausted. It had to rest, gather its strength, so it waited.

Pete was in his little office, munching on a vast tub of sweet popcorn and watching a really cheesy black-and-white movie version of *Frankenstein*. The Monster was being brought back to life by massive surges of electricity.

'People don't come back to life,' he muttered, taking a quick swig of cooling coffee. Then he jumped as he heard a couple of thumps.

He turned. They seemed to be coming from the body room.

There were a couple more.

'Ted?' But Ted had gone off duty about an hour ago. 'Ted, that you?'

No answer, just another thump.

Frowning, Pete got up and walked out of his office and into the body room. The thumping started again, furiously.

Pete flicked the light switch, bathing the room in a harsh fluorescent white.

The thumping was coming from inside one of the morgue containers. Which one?

It was Number Eight, he realised. The one with their mysterious John Doe. Tentatively he reached out, flicking the catch . . .

The door sprung open, almost ripped off its hinges by the violence of the movement. The gurney shot out, propelling the dead body forward and across the room, where it thudded into the opposite wall.

Pete did a double-take, unable to believe his eyes. His credulity was stretched further when the dead body groaned and staggered up.

The final straw that broke the proverbial camel's back came however, when Pete really looked at the body. It was wrapped in the shroud, the John Doe tag still attached to the right big toe, but the body was of a different man. It was taller, younger, with wild hair.

The bizarre apparition staggered towards Pete, who suddenly felt very warm. His legs felt like jelly and he wanted to cry out, but all he could manage was a hiss.

Everything went black.

Bruce Gerhardt was snoring, keeping his wife wide awake, as usual.

Miranda Gerhardt was used to her husband's snores — they had been married over five years — but that did not mean she liked them.

Miranda stared at the clock. Bruce had got home from the hospital at around ten thirty, murmuring something about someone being shot in Chinatown. After fourteen years as a paramedic, she thought, he ought to have got used to horrible injuries by now, but then again, that was Bruce. A carer, someone who would inconvenience himself without a thought if it would help someone else.

She was lucky to be married to such a nice man, she reminded herself.

If only he didn't snore so much.

On the floor, just beside the wardrobe, Bruce had placed his plastic Medikit bag.

For a brief moment, it glowed green, and when that faded, a small hole had been melted through it, from the inside.

Something oozed out of the new hole, something green and essentially amorphous. Its normally fluid texture had taken on an almost chitinous appearance. It slumped on to the floor, desperately trying to inch forward. Already it could feel the Master's life-force ebbing. The mental stress on the Master was terrible and so it drove itself forward. It needed something organic to dissipate into, to wrap its DNA around and combine with, providing the Master with a better form, a more suitable host body.

Rearing up, tiny flakes of hard skin chipping off, the creature jumped forward, landing on the soft coverings over the sleeping humans.

The male was nearer, and something inside drove it on. Perhaps the Master preferred a male form.

The male human's mouth was wide open, which made oozing inside easy. For a brief moment it felt the human gagging and dying. That was of consequence because now it felt renewed, strong. Its task was almost complete. It filled outwards, its body becoming one with the dead human, revitalising the vital organs as best it could. It was now aware that the Master was getting stronger.

The last thing it was conscious of was that the Master, however, was displeased – this body would not work for long. It needed a proper Time Lord body, not something as primitive as a human. It needed two hearts, a respiratory by-pass system and a lower body temperature. But there was nothing more it could do now except keep this body animated long enough for the Master to find a Time Lord's body to inhabit.

Then it dissipated for ever.

Miranda Gerhardt sighed contentedly. Bruce had stopped snoring. She rolled over and snuggled up behind him, and began to drift to sleep, content with her wonderful husband who loved her just as much as she loved him.

The new millennium was going to be just wonderful.

★ ★ ★

The man in white had fainted. Why?

He reached down to feel for the man in white's pulse but suddenly whipped his hand back, as if he'd been burned.

His hand. Hands. He looked at them.

'Not my hands,' he murmured.

What did that mean? Why weren't they his hands? What were his real hands like? He could not remember, yet something told him this was wrong.

He was cold; the room was very chilly. He needed warmth and some clothes. He felt exposed and unprotected – but what did he need protection from?

He staggered into the corridor, and looked out of a window.

Dark. Rain. Cold.

Where was he? What was he doing here?

He opened a door that was clearly marked *NO ENTRY* but, for some reason, that did not seem to matter. The room was cold but full of things. Big things.

Beds, they were called beds. Yes, he could remember that. They were piled on top of each other, and the room was quite dark. There was some scaffolding in one corner.

This room was being redecorated.

It was a hospital – that's right. A hospital.

What was he doing in a hospital? Had he had

an accident that meant his hands had been cut off? Was that why they felt strange? That aside, his whole body felt strange, as if it did not really belong to him at all.

He turned to a window. There was a light outside. Lots of lights. It was a place they parked cars in. Whatever a car was. Why couldn't he remember?

The light meant that he could see himself reflected in the window.

He could not remotely remember what his reflection ought to have been, but whoever it was staring back at him struck absolutely no chords of recognition.

'You're not me,' he mumbled. 'Who are you?'

Suddenly, he felt very tired and very dizzy. He staggered back, and sat on a bed that was lying clear of the others.

'You're not me,' he repeated. 'But who am I?'

That was the question he really needed an answer to. Nothing seemed remotely familiar at all. And that frightened him.

He looked about him, at the shadows cast upon the wall by the outside lights; at the door to the bright corridor; at the window itself, where he could still see a faint image of (he presumed) his own face.

He tried to get up again, but his legs were tired and instead he just fell to the floor.

Curling up into a foetal ball, he hugged himself to keep warm. 'Who am I?' he said again.

And inside his brain the words echoed over and over again.

Who am I?

One for sorrow,
two for joy

To millions of people all over the world, the breaking of this particular dawn signified the start of a very important day. It was December 31st, 1999. New Year's Eve. Whether in the bright lights of Times Square, the ancient charm of Trafalgar Square, the exquisite beauty of La Place du Concord or the dignified austerity of Red Square, people would, later this day, be celebrating the ending of the millennium. And looking forward to the twenty-first century.

For Dr Grace Holloway, still dressed in her now crumpled ballgown, it began drearily. She woke up and heaved her face up off her desk and tried to massage some life into her right cheek. It had taken the full weight of her sleeping head all night, and she imagined that someone could jab a needle right through it and she would still not feel a thing.

Wiping at her eyes, she yawned and stared hard at the X-ray still lit by the light-box. She glanced at her desk clock: 6.30 a.m. Last time she had looked it had said 4.10 a.m. Surely she had not been sleeping for two hours? She had work to do.

Her telephone rang twice – an internal call. Wearily she picked it up, expecting it to be Roger Swift, remonstrating with her about her mysterious patient's death.

It was Pete from the morgue, going on about the living dead and damage done to the mortuary room by some drunk. As her head cleared, Grace realised that Pete was talking about her deceased patient's cold room.

Still not entirely clear what he was going on about, Grace agreed to take a wander down to the morgue – on the proviso she could get some coffee on the way.

After replacing the receiver, Grace dragged herself out of her chair (God, that was uncomfortable to sleep in; her back would probably be protesting for days) and staggered towards the office door. She threw on her white coat, as if it would protect her from the evil spells that Pete was convinced had brought someone back to life. She'd get some breakfast first, and then see what was on the porter's mind. She certainly could not concentrate without some food inside her.

The object of Pete's consternation watched from a corridor as the porter dashed away, having just finished a telephone conversation about some incident in the mortuary.

That seemed vaguely familiar, but he could not put a finger on exactly why. Had he seen something? Something about a door?

Whatever it was, he would find out soon, no doubt. If only he could clear this strange fog in his brain. He had tried sleeping, but despite feeling exceptionally tired, his mind simply would not let him go under. Instead, it had kept probing, kept digging, trying to find answers to impossible questions. Who am I? Why am I here? Where am I going? Philosophically or geographically?

By now he had wandered into the mortuary itself, and immediately saw the damaged container door, battered and hanging off its hinges, indentations made by a fast moving gurney no doubt.

How did he know that? Anything could have made those marks, yet the size, shape and amount of damage generally indicated something hitting it at a high speed. Internally – the door was definitely damaged from inside.

For a brief moment he had a glimpse in his mind's eye of the door springing open, seeing the astonished porter's face staring at him.

Could it have been him inside the cold room?

He looked down at his feet, a tag attached to his right big toe. He was wearing a grey shroud. Hmmm?

One thing he was becoming aware of was that he was starting to get cold. Where could he find better garments?

The faint noise of a television (now, how did he recognise those sounds?) could be heard through another door. He gingerly walked towards the noises and discovered a small office just off a locker room. Sure enough, a television was playing. Cartoons. He watched for a moment as a blue cat chased a mouse around the corner of a house, and then crashed into a rake. The rake sprang up, smacking the cat right in the face and . . .

Violence.

He shook his head, despairingly. Cartoons or real life, something inside him was twisting at the thought of wanton violence. It was something wrong. Something he had to stop . . . why? Why did he think that?

He needed to get away, out of the claustrophobic hospital, with its smell of antiseptic and brightly lit corridors. He needed open spaces, trees and grass. Birds and animals. Natural things.

He needed the TARDIS as well.

TARDIS? What exactly was the TARDIS?

Oh, well, whatever it was, he guessed that he would know it when he found it.

He began to rummage through some of the open lockers. Theft was not exactly moral either, but these clothes were not being used and he reasoned that he could return them later. Perhaps the TARDIS had a wardrobe where he could find his own clothes.

The first locker he opened had a pile of clothes neatly folded inside a couple of plastic bags, marked with the name Walker General Hospital. He could see a rather shabby tweed sports coat, hideous leather patches on the elbows. A pair of loud check pants and a white shirt. They looked very familiar, but obviously would not fit him. They were the clothes of a much smaller man. Perched on top of the pile was a straw hat. He reached out and touched it and something in his mind clicked. He could suddenly see someone wearing the hat, indeed all these clothes, standing outside a large blue box. The place was dark, but the small man was holding a strange casket of some sort. Something else familiar . . .

He let go of the hat and the vision vanished. He picked up the hat again, but this time nothing happened. Nevertheless, it had given him some information. He decided he would keep the hat, just in case.

The next locker contained a costume of some sort, encased in a special plastic clothing wrap, hanging neatly. It was stamped *Berman's Costumiers and Fancy Dress Hire (San Francisco) Inc.* He quite liked the look of the grey velvet cravat with its gold stud which was stuffed at the bottom of the bag. He opened another locker, then another and another. If he took something from each of these fancy dress items, he might get away with it. He reached for one containing a large dark brown frock coat . . .

Chang Lee was perched on the top of a burned out Chevvie that had been dumped a few months ago behind the chain-link fence that bordered Rose Street.

He could see the big blue box, surrounded by police tape in Rose Alley, just on the other side of the street. The police had departed, presumably having carted off the bodies of both Pik Sim and Lin Wang.

In his hands was the bag containing the strange man's things. He was looking at the gold pocket watch; might be worth quite a bit. The long, silver thing that might have been a torch seemed worthless, but the shield-shaped key, was that the key to the blue box?

Chang Lee slid off the car and hurried down Rose Avenue and into Rose Alley. He checked no one could see him and wandered up to the police line, glancing briefly at the white outlines on the ground that marked out where the three bodies had fallen.

He ducked under the tape and went straight to the door. *POLICE PUBLIC CALL BOX,* it said across the top. On one of the panels on the wooden door were various instructions on how to telephone for the police, in case of an emergency. Whatever this was, it was certainly bizarre. But if it belonged to the cops, was the little man a police officer? A private investigator perhaps, or one of those weirdos who worked at the DA's office?

Chang Lee touched the box, and whipped his hand back in surprise. It was vibrating very slightly, letting out an almost imperceptible hum that he had to strain to hear.

This was no ordinary box. He looked at the key in his hand – even if it was the key to the box, it might be booby trapped. Having survived last night's attempt by the other gang to wipe him out, he was not particularly keen on getting blown apart by a DA's box.

'One for *The X Files*,' he muttered, pocketing the key and walking slowly away. This needed more thought.

Miranda Gerhardt was awoken by the noise of her husband closing a drawer next to their wardrobe.

She glanced sleepily over at the green LED figures on their bedside clock – it was 8.45.

'Bit early, darling,' she murmured.

Bruce did not reply. He was standing, apparently gazing at himself in the full-length mirror on the inside of the wardrobe door. He had evidently showered because his beautiful black hair was perfectly gelled and slicked back – normally it stuck up in ridiculous directions first thing in the morning. Discarded on the floor was the shirt he had noisily retrieved from the drawer. She stared hard at his naked back and smiled at his gorgeous body, muscles toned, skin tanned.

When they'd met five years earlier, he'd recently been divorced from his first wife. Miranda had been in a car accident and Bruce had looked after her in the ambulance, where they had struck up a friendship. In a totally fairy-tale romance sort of way, they had wined and dined each other after she had recovered. He had been kind, sincere and attentive; her reciprocal attention had massaged his self-confidence back into shape, proving to him – and to Miranda – that he really was the perfect man.

Bruce was still gazing at the mirror, and Miranda slid slightly across to his side of the bed, trying to catch his reflection in the glass.

His side of the bed was cold – he must have been up for a good half hour. Still unable to see his face, she spoke softly.

'Hi, honey.'

'This body won't last long,' Bruce whispered.

'Another few years yet, Bruce. I'll still love you when you're wrinkled and chubby.' Miranda went back to her warmer side of the bed, wrapping the quilt around her tightly.

Bruce just ignored her.

'I need the Doctor's body,' he sighed.

Miranda grinned and sat up, then got on to her knees, still tugging the quilt round her. 'You could do with a body that doesn't snore, sure, but you don't need a doctor.' She stifled a yawn. 'C'mon honey, let's get back to bed.'

Bruce did not turn, but spoke louder. 'My name isn't "honey".'

Miranda giggled. 'What should I call you, then?'

'"Master" will do.'

Smiling, Miranda stepped off the bed, letting the quilt fall to the floor. She tiptoed up behind him and slid her arms around his waist, snuggling her head against the back of his neck. 'All right. "Master", come back to bed!'

Bruce turned to face her and the first thing that went through her mind was that he was not smiling. That, and the fact that his eyes were suddenly bright green, shining and slightly elliptic. Large dark pupils in a sea of luminescence.

The next thing that went through her mind was that Bruce's right hand was round her throat, cutting off her voice, her air. She tried to kick out, to struggle but realised he had lifted her off the ground. She was blacking out.

The last thing that went through Miranda Gerhardt's mind was that her lovely, beautiful, perfect

Bruce was trying to throttle her. Deliberately. She coughed and then suddenly felt very light-headed.

Had Bruce let go? Was the game over? Was she –

The Master let the woman drop as he turned back to the wardrobe. He rummaged inside for a while, finding a pair of quality denim jeans and a check shirt. He quickly put them on, adding a pair of light boots to the combination.

Slung over a chair by the bed was the black paramedic's jerkin that his host body wore the night before. Yes, he had been in the ambulance, and had taken the Doctor to that hospital. He ought to be able to retrace this 'Bruce''s steps, and use his identity to track down his old enemy.

He looked down at Bruce's medical bag and decided it might be appropriate to carry it.

The Master touched his new skin. It was only human and was like walking around in a cadaver. Before too long it would begin to decompose as any dead human would.

He needed a Time Lord body to inhabit, and he knew exactly where to find one, freshly injured or dead, that he could utilise with no future problems.

He smiled for the first time as he put on a pair of dark glasses to hide his eyes, the last remnant of the morphic carrier he had ingested prior to his extermination by the Daleks. The Master knew then it would protect him long enough to find some kind of sanctuary. He picked up the medical bag and left the apartment, confident that if anyone saw him it would be just reliable old Bruce Gerhardt on his way to work.

'What a nice man,' they would say.

Pete was pointing at the wrecked door while Grace was examining the damaged gurney. 'It simply wasn't the same guy, Dr Holloway.'

Grace stood up, running a hand through her strawberry-blonde hair and shrugged. Her hunger had been sated by a large bowl of muesli and three cups of decaf, but she still could not get her head around Pete's weird story.

'Strikes me, Pete, that you saw the guy who stole the body.'

Pete shook his head. 'No way. He was wearing a shroud, and that JD tag on his toe!'

Grace folded her arms and looked Pete directly in the eye. 'Somehow, I don't believe that the Second Coming is likely to happen here.'

'Yeah, right.' Pete smiled for the first time. 'He'd go to a better hospital.'

He went to go back to his office, but then turned back to Grace. 'I know what I saw.'

Grace just smiled. 'Yeah, okay Pete. Pop by psychiatric on your way home. Pick up some more mind-altering drugs, all right?'

Pete turned away, muttering.

Grace smiled and headed back for her office. Pete and Ted were known for their bizarre sense of humour, usually aided by copious amounts of cider that mysteriously vanished whenever Roger Swift tried to pin something on them.

Then again, something had done a lot of damage to that door, and Pete certainly had the symptoms of a sudden faint rather than unconsciousness induced by alcohol.

Why was everything involving her mysterious (and now vanished) corpse always so complicated?

She called the elevator that would take her back up the ground floor and her office. She was still thinking about the strength needed to rip a sealed morgue door off its hinges like that, when the doors opened and she got in.

The first thing that greeted her when the doors reopened was a long line of out-patients or relatives waiting for this morning's Emergency Room business. Walking towards her was Shelly Curtis, looking remarkably fresh, presumably having caught a few hours more sleep than Grace had. She was relieving the receptionist, and as she settled down, Grace leaned across the desk.

'Can you believe this? Some creep's made off with that John Doe from last night.'

Curtis screwed her face up in disgust. 'Eeew! Body-snatchers.'

Watching this exchange, the stranger recognised the tall strawberry-blonde from somewhere. But where?

For a moment he suddenly saw her, gowned and masked, as if leaning over him. He looked around himself now. If he was in a hospital, perhaps he had had an accident. That might explain why he could remember very little, and why even his own face seemed unfamiliar.

He had to talk to her. He stood up from the line of patients and headed towards the reception desk. He stopped in his tracks when the blonde woman began talking to another man who hurried over, telling the receptionist not to call the police.

'But Dr Swift, if someone's stolen a body . . . ?' she said, but this Dr Swift shook his head. Then he turned to the blonde doctor.

'Dr Holloway,' he was saying (so that was her name; store that. Well, try to remember it, at least). 'Dr Holloway, can you give me some of your valuable time?'

Time.

That was it. Or was it? Something to do with time?

He glanced over at the clock on the wall.

10.22 a.m., it read. December 31st.

Grace allowed herself to be escorted into her own office by the hospital's administrator, slightly bewildered by his haste.

'Roger,' she tried to say, 'Roger, we have to call the police, because –'

He held his hand up, cutting her off, crossing to the X-rays still on her light-box. 'We don't need to advertise our mistakes, do we?'

He took the X-rays down.

Grace frowned. 'What are you saying?'

Swift looked out of her office and then back at her, a false smile on his face. He held up the X-rays. 'Two hearts, Grace. No wonder you got lost in there.'

'Exactly.'

'Or,' he said, still smiling, using that look Grace knew he reserved for dying elderly patients who wanted to donate their life's savings to his hospital, 'maybe this really is a double exposure. Jim Salinger seems to think so.'

'Jim Salinger would,' Grace retorted. 'He has about as much imagination as a mouse and half the guts to say what he really thinks.'

'Nevertheless, Grace, I can't afford to lose you.' Swift took a pair of scissors off Grace's desktop.

Grace reached out, grabbing his hand, frowning. 'What are you going to do?'

'What you should have done last night.' Swift neatly cut the X-rays in half, quarters, then eighths

72

and dropped the scissors back on her desk. He placed the fragments of the X-rays into his pocket. 'I'll be visiting the furnace soon, I think. Just to be certain.'

Grace stared open mouthed. Then she stepped back towards the wall in bewilderment. 'Am I having a bad dream here? I lose a patient, then his body, and now you destroy the only proof –'

Swift held up his hand to stop her, still smiling insincerely. 'That you were careless.'

'That I had no way of knowing,' she continued angrily. 'That he had –'

'Stop.' Swift stopped smiling, and scowled. Sincerely. 'A man died last night because you lost your way.'

'You bet I did!' Grace was nearly shouting. She reached across, slamming her office door shut. 'You've seen those X-rays. The guy had two hearts!'

'But now, without a body, and without any records, no one need ever know he was here. I've already spoken to Salinger and Wheeler. I'll talk to Curtis.'

'And Pete and Ted? And Bruce and Joey in the ambulance? And Lana on reception last night? And the police officers and everyone else who knew that he was here?'

Swift just shrugged. 'Just let me take care of this, Grace.'

'No!'

'Believe me, this is the best way for all of us.'

Grace sat down hard, shocked at Swift's proposal, but confidant that he could do it. Even bribery was cheaper than the fiasco that would erupt if it got out. Rationally she could see that. But this was illegal. As big a malpractice as the one Swift was implying she had committed by killing the mysterious man. 'But Roger, what was he? How can we learn from him? I have to find that body and –'

Roger Swift slammed his fist down hard on the desk, and Grace jumped in alarm.

'And I have to keep Walker General open, Grace. At all costs.'

Grace shook her head. 'No.' She swallowed hard and looked him in the eye.

'No, Dr Swift. If you do this, I'll quit.'

'You don't mean that.'

Grace just stared at him.

Grace looked up at the clock in reception as she struggled towards the elevator, her arms full of boxes of papers. Perched on top was a small plastic Mickey Mouse – a gift from her colleagues on her last birthday.

The elevator doors opened, and she stepped in. The Mickey Mouse toppled off and bounced on to the floor – and straight into the hands of a

74

bizarre looking man. He got into the lift with her, and replaced the toy on top of the boxes.

Grace muttered a thanks and stared at the indicator as it went past Lower Ground, Basement and finally Sub–Basement, where the parking lot was.

The doors opened, and Grace was puzzled to see the man follow her out.

He tapped her on the shoulder, and her heart began to race. This was all she needed right now – her alarm was in her bag, but her hands were full.

'Puccini!' The man smiled.

Grace looked at him. He was in his mid-thirties, at a guess. He had rather sad looking eyes, yet they were bright blue and quite attractive. He had a nice bone structure and a wonderful smile, showing a full set of good teeth. He was about her height, but with swept back hair that looked as if he'd licked his fingers and jammed them into a light socket.

It was his clothes that made her frown. He was dressed like something out of a Victorian movie. A long-tailed chocolate brown frock-coat, a wing-collared shirt and grey velvet cravat. He also wore a fawn paisley vest, and grey pants. His feet were completely bare which meant, Grace thought, they must have been feeling the cold from the rough concrete floor.

'Going to a party, are we?' she suggested.

The stranger just carried on smiling. 'We've met before.'

'I don't think so.' Grace began walking towards her car.

'I do.' He reached out to take one of the boxes but Grace pulled back and the Mickey Mouse took another tumble. Again he scooped it up, holding it out to her. 'I know you – you're tired of life. But afraid of dying.'

Grace speeded up, willing to sacrifice her Mouse if it meant she could get away from some Englishman who had either had too much to drink at a pre-millennium party or was an escapee from Psychiatric.

'There was music,' he called after her. '*Madame Butterfly.* And you were there. I saw you. Last night!'

Maybe he'd seen her at the Opera House, and followed her out. God, somehow she'd picked up a stalker. Wonderful.

She dumped the boxes on the hood of her car, but remembering her self-defence classes, did not get the key from her bag. Don't turn your back on him, Grace, she remembered.

The man was still standing some way away. He was scratching at his chest, unbuttoning his vest.

'I don't know who I am, but I know you do!'

This gets worse and worse, thought Grace. A

drunken stalker ready to expose himself. The year 2000 could only be an improvement on this.

'Please,' she shouted. 'Just go away, or I'll call security.'

'You're my only hope,' he yelled back. 'Do you know who I am?'

Grace slowly opened her bag, keeping an eye on the man. She felt the alarm. Next to it, her keys. They were the better option. She felt them in her clenched fist, and began to feel calmer. She lifted them out, transferring them to her other hand and fumbled behind her, searching for the keyhole.

'I have no idea who you are,' she said. 'I have never seen you before in my life.' The key slotted in. 'Now leave me alone!'

The man stepped forward. 'Please help me. You're a doctor –'

'*Was* a doctor. My oath just expired.' Grace heard the central locking click and hauled her door open. With one hand she hurled her bag on to the passenger seat and grabbed the boxes off the hood and into the back. Seconds later she was seated, and at a push of a button, the four doors centrally locked again.

She started the car up and glanced outside. He stalker had disappeared, hopefully having taken the hint.

She had just begun to ease the car out of its

parking space when something landed on her skirt. She looked down to see the plastic Mickey Mouse. Peering into her rear-view mirror, she could see the stalker in the back seat, his piercing blue eyes staring back at her.

Grace finally gave in. She screamed and slammed her fist down on the horn, letting out an elongated noise, trying to catch the parking lot attendant's attention, wherever he was.

'Get out of my car!' she screamed.

'My hearts!' The man in the back screamed even louder, and doubled up. 'There's something here!'

Fascinated and unable to take it all in, Grace turned and looked. The stalker had ripped his shirt open, revealing a well-developed body, rising and falling sharply – he was having difficulty breath-ing.

Then she saw what he was protesting about. Sticking out of his chest was a tiny piece of wire – or at least it looked like wire. Yet, as realisation dawned, Grace still could not accept what she was seeing.

'What is it?' The man was clearly in agony.

'Oh, God,' murmured Grace, 'it can't be . . .'

The man grabbed at it and, accompanied by a screech of pain, he wrenched it out of his body, letting it flop to the floor.

'Two hearts,' he gasped. 'I have two hearts.

Please, get me out of here, before they kill me again —'

He slumped forward, banging his head on her headrest and then crashing down on the back seat, apparently unconscious.

'Please,' he said, so quietly she almost missed it. 'You've got to help me.'

Just as the parking lot attendant and a security officer from the hospital rushed through a door from behind them, Grace slammed the car into Drive and sped out of the parking lot.

Three storeys above the parking lot, Shelly Curtis was flicking through her Armistead Maupin novel, idly waiting for the next emergency to arrive, when she was aware that someone was staring down at her.

She glanced up and smiled. 'Hi Bruce, what's with the shades?'

'I had a bad night.'

Curtis nodded. 'Yeah, and I bet Miranda gave you a darn good telling off as well.' She poked at him with a pen. 'And I bet you deserved it.' She looked down at her receptionist notebook. 'You're not on shift for a few more hours. Why don't you go home and sleep it off.'

'That might be . . . difficult.'

Curtis laughed. 'Ha! She's thrown you out for the day, right! Score one for the sisterhood.'

Bruce did not laugh. Or smile. He just stared at her through his dark glasses.

'Did you want something?' she asked him.

'What happened to the gunshot wound we brought in last night? I've got orders to move him.'

Curtis shook her head. 'Sorry, Bruce. He died.'

'Yeah. They wanted me to get his body.'

Curtis thought this was a little odd. Why would a paramedic want to take a stiff anywhere? That was Pete or Ted's job. And who asked Bruce to do this anyway? Perhaps she ought to just check with –

Bruce was picking at one of his fingernails, when it just came clean off. He flicked it away.

'You okay, Bruce?'

'Where is it?' he snapped back.

Curtis decided this was none of her business. Miranda had obviously put Bruce in a bad mood and, fingernails or not, she was not going to get involved. 'The body's gone,' she said simply. 'Stolen.'

Bruce seemed to take this in his stride. 'Of course. If he died then he regenerated.'

Curtis did not understand any of this. Bruce was acting very strangely.

'Okay,' said Bruce. 'Where are his things?'

'The kid you brought with you stole them from Grace Holloway's office.'

Bruce cocked his head, as if thinking something through. 'The Asian child.'

Curtis was perturbed by Bruce's unusual tone. 'Yeah, the "Asian" child.' She stared harder at him. 'Bruce, I think you must be really sick.'

Bruce suddenly smiled. 'Thank you,' he said, turned on his heel and marched out.

Curtis decided to call Mr Prentiss, Bruce's superintendent. Her friend was acting real weird this morning, and she thought his boss ought to know.

Grace's condominium was quite a walk from where she had parked the car. Slightly embarrassed at this, she refused to let the stranger carry anything, because of his injuries. Despite that, he kept up right behind her and before long, she was unlocking her apartment door, carefully undoing each of the five locks in order.

'You all right?' she asked as the door swung open.

'Much better,' replied her charge.

'Good.'

'Especially now that I don't have a piece of primitive wiring inside my cardiovascular system.' He dropped the micro-probe on to a small cabinet beside the front door.

Grace wandered into her living room, ready to dump the boxes on one of her armchairs.

Instead, she faced an almost empty room, with a naked bulb swinging slightly from the ceiling. The only furniture left was an armchair and a coffee table. 'I don't believe it. He's taken all his stuff.'

'Who?'

'Brian.'

'Your . . . boyfriend?' he said hesitantly, as if he was unsure if that was the right terminology.

'Ex-boyfriend.' Grace flopped into the armchair. 'Apparently.' She sighed. 'Open your shirt again. I want to listen to your heart.'

'Hearts,' he corrected.

'Whatever.'

The stranger looked for somewhere to sit.

Grace groaned. 'He took the sofa. The miserable little —'

The stranger was looking around, and pointed at a print of the Mona Lisa on one of the walls. 'He left you that.' He walked towards it. 'Leonardo had a terrible cold when he painted this.'

'How can you tell?'

He smiled back at Grace. 'I helped out. Made a few improvements of my own.' He stopped. 'Now how come I remember that?'

Grace wondered if the trauma of whatever had happened to him (and God help her, she could not begin to explain what exactly that was) was affecting his mind more than before. Delirium.

She pointed to a short set of stairs, leading to a raised bedroom. 'We can sit up there. Come on.'

Moments later, they were seated on the bed, the stranger having undone his shirt again. Grace had her stethoscope out and was placing it over his heart.

He was ignoring her, looking out of the window across the city. He could see the famous Golden Gate Bridge and beyond it, the Marin Headlands.

'San Francisco. I've never been here while it's still inhabited. What a lovely view.'

Grace ignored him. 'Maybe,' she said putting the stethoscope in her ears, 'you've had selective amnesia brought on by shock.'

'Maybe. I can't remember.'

Grace began listening to his heartbeat. 'Shh.' She sat up. 'You're still fibrillating badly.'

'No, I'm not. Here.' He moved the stethoscope over to the other side of his chest.

'Oh, God . . .' Grace let go of the stethoscope.

'See,' the stranger said. 'It's not an echo.'

'Two hearts.' She looked him in the eye. 'You were right. Who are you?'

The stranger got up, and began rooting through her CD collection. 'I was dead for too long this time. Your anaesthetic almost destroyed the regenerative process.'

He suddenly smiled and waved a CD at her,

changing the subject in a breath. '*Turandot*. Poor Puccini – I was with him, you know. When he died. It was so sad that he never got the chance to finish it. I offered, but everyone else preferred Alfano's work, and so he did it, based on Puccini's notes, of course.'

Grace removed the CD from his hand. 'Yeah, right.'

She cleared her throat, and decided to treat this like any other illness, despite both the peculiarity of the problem and the patient. 'I'm going to take a blood sample and find out what's going on here.'

The stranger shook his head. 'No, Grace, you don't understand. I have thirteen lives, twelve attempts at getting it right.'

'So,' Grace smiled. 'So, you're trying to tell me that you came back from the dead?'

He looked at her in complete seriousness. 'Of course not. The dead stay dead. I regenerated, eventually.'

'I'm sorry,' she stood up. 'You can't turn back time.'

The stranger suddenly beamed, and Grace saw something beautiful in his eyes. Eyes so full of life whereas they had been so pained, so ill just half an hour earlier. 'Yes you can, Grace.'

'I'm not a child,' she snapped without meaning to. 'Don't talk to me like one. Only children believe that crap. I'm a doctor!'

The stranger took her hand, and she found she did not mind as much as she felt she ought to. 'But it was a child's dream that made you want to be a doctor, wasn't it?'

Grace was suddenly back at her parent's house in Sacramento, watching as an elderly doctor left their bedroom, shaking his head at her father.

Daddy had gripped little Grace's hand tightly and she could see he was crying. She cried too, not really knowing why, but realising that the doctor who had been looking after Mummy had looked sad too.

'Mummy's gone away, angel,' Daddy had said. 'She's not coming back, I'm afraid. Dr Seinkewicz did what he could.'

And although she could not really understand what Dr Seinkewicz could not have done, she knew that one day she would have to be a doctor and find out.

Here she was, nearly thirty years later and they'd still not found a complete cure for cancer. But Grace had become a doctor and had made sure that a lot more five-year-olds still had their mothers and fathers to go home with at the end of the day.

She was back in her condo, staring at the wonderful blue eyes of her mysterious patient.

He looked away, back out towards the Golden Gate Bridge. 'Don't be sad, Grace,' he murmured. 'You will do great things.'

★ ★ ★

Chang Lee had kicked around a bit in the neighbourhood, avoiding other people but always staying within easy reach of the tall blue box.

After a while, he had seen a patrol car drive up the alley, park and then drive away again. Perhaps they had been looking for him. The hospital must have reported him by now.

Now the coast was clear and he dashed over to the box, ducking under the tape once again. This time, the key was read, and he was going to use it.

He twisted it in the door and as it opened, the hum got louder.

He had expected a tiny little box room, just large enough for him to stand in. What greeted him was impossible.

Beautiful, but impossible.

The room was like the inside of one of those huge ancient houses he had seen on television once, in some old British *Masterpiece Theatre* show.

Everything was made of intricately carved wood with lacquered panels. Brass switches dominated a huge mushroom shaped object at the centre of the room and when he looked up, he could see a high, domed ceiling through the gloom.

It was not very bright and Chang Lee nervously spoke into the darkness. 'Hello?'

There was no reply. He looked back at the central shape and realised it was on a slight, rounded, platform, with four sets of double steps leading up to it. A brass rail surrounded it, and on the side nearest him, a tiny screen was flickering.

CRITICAL TIMING MALFUNCTION
AUTOMATIC EMERGENCY LANDING
  INSTIGATED
EARTH
UNITED STATES OF AMERICA
SAN FRANCISCO
LOCAL DATELINE 1999

This was the only light in the room, apart from that which came through the marble and wood doors from the outside.

'This is too weird,' Chang Lee decided. He was going to turn back and go out when the doors slammed shut.

Chang Lee saw two tiny pinpricks of green light moving towards him. They got bigger – they looked like eyes. Then they vanished suddenly.

Before he could relax, Chang Lee realised that someone was actually standing in the shadows where the green lights had been. The figure walked towards him. As his eyes grew more accustomed to the light and the figure got nearer, Chang Lee called out again.

'Who's there?'

'You don't want to know,' came the reply, and the figure became recognisable.

'Hey, Bruce,' Chang Lee said. 'Man, you scared me. This place is freaky enough, yeah?'

Bruce was standing quite still, his head slightly cocked to one side. He was still wearing his black paramedic's jerkin but underneath it he wore a black tunic with a Nehru collar, and black trousers and boots. All three items of clothing seemed to be made out of the same material, which looked a bit like snake-skin. Although there was not a great deal of light, as Bruce took a step forward, the snake-skin effect rippled slightly, almost as if the clothes were alive. Chang Lee decided he looked quite weird and took a step back.

Bruce seemed to look at him through his dark glasses and then ignored him, walking past him and up one of the tiny steps, past the railing, and touched the central shape. Then he turned back.

'Lee.' Bruce's voice sounded very strange. Almost as if he had hurt his jaw and was trying to get it working again. 'Chang Lee. Isn't that your name?'

Chang Lee moved towards him, up one of the other sets of steps.

Immediately the whole chamber was flooded in light, and the tall central shape began to light up as well, like a Christmas tree.

'Well, well. The TARDIS likes you, Chang Lee.'

Chang Lee looked around at the marvellous room he was in. The whole box was bigger on the inside than the outside.

'Yes,' said Bruce. 'It's dimensionally transcendental.'

Chang Lee nodded. 'Yeah. Like, right.' He looked back at Bruce. 'What d'you mean, "the TARDIS likes me", Bruce?'

Bruce smiled suddenly, and removed his shades. His eyes were fierce green light. The ones he had seen earlier.

'I am not Bruce, my young friend. I merely inhabit his body.'

Chang Lee realised that something had happened. Bruce was really ill. 'Oh, yeah. So, er, who are you really?'

Bruce stepped closer. 'You really want to know, do you?'

Chang Lee was captivated by those eyes. They seemed to bore right into him, deep deep down, as if they could see everything inside him, his whole life. Every experience, every feeling. Happy. Sad. Angry. Hurt. Chang Lee wanted to close his own eyes, shut out Bruce's horrible new green ones, but he simply could not.

He dug his fingernails into the palms of his hands until they really hurt. Suddenly he managed to shake his head, feeling as if he had broken free of something.

He stepped back. 'Stop that! Bruce, hell man, if you're not Bruce, what are you?'

'I am known as the Master.'

Bruce, or the Master, pointed at the key Chang Lee was holding.

'Where is he?'

'Who?' Chang Lee frowned. 'Oh, the guy who had this before? He died. All his stuff is mine now.'

'No,' said the Master. 'No, he's not dead. But he has stolen my body.'

'But –'

The Master suddenly frowned and staggered, as if he as hurting. 'I . . . I will die unless we bring him back here.' He looked up at Chang Lee, pleading. 'You have to help me get my own body back.'

Chang Lee stared at the Master, then at the fantastic room all around him. 'Yeah, right. And what's in it for me?'

The Master just smiled. 'You? You get to live.'

Three for a girl

Grace had been working for the whole day now, adrenalin providing her with the energy that would normally have faded ages before. It had been a long time since she had missed her regulation six hours' sleep, and she knew she would pay for it later.

She had dragged the kitchen table up into the bedroom and set up her medical equipment all over it, as if trying to fit the entire contents of one of Walker General's well-stocked labs on to a space roughly three feet square.

She had allowed herself the luxury of changing out of her ballgown after a quick shower, and now sat hunched over a microscope in a pair of black Levi's, a tight cerise Versace Profumi blouse and a pair of black Doc Martens shoes.

The strange man had requested a shower and asked if Grace could lend him a pair of socks and shoes – saying that if he did not keep his feet warm, he would soon get a cold. Aware of how delicate he must currently be, Grace had dug out a pair of Brian's old brown shoes that he used in winter for tramping about in snow or mud. As such, they were stained and scuffed and Brian had obviously abandoned them during his hurried departure.

'They fit,' she heard the strange man mutter after a while. She glanced up to see him sitting on the steps leading up to her bed area, polishing the shoes with an old duster. They now looked brand new.

'Good,' she grunted. 'Keep 'em.'

'Thanks. What d'you think of my blood?'

Grace looked up from her microscope and sighed, running a weary hand through her hair. 'Well, it's not just blood –'

The stranger was pacing up and down the steps, muttering. 'Maybe if I walk about in them for a while, they'll stretch and I'll get used to them.'

Grace watched him for a moment, and then looked back at the impossibility she had on her slide under the microscope. Some fresh air would do her a lot of good right now.

'That's a good idea. Let's go for a walk,' she said, getting up and grabbing her coat from over the back of the armchair.

The strange man beamed, his eyes sparkling. 'A brisk December walk in the park in the evening. Just what the doctor ordered, as they say.'

'Yeah. Right.' Grace found him a scarf from the same pile of Brian-rejects and went to find a woolly hat.

When she came back, he was staring at the microscope. 'I'm sure I used to have a laboratory full of things like this. I think. Somehow it just brought some memories back, but they're still all jumbled up.'

He suddenly looked very crestfallen. 'I hope my memory comes back before too long. It's very inconvenient, you know.'

Typical British understatement, Grace thought. She tossed him a red woolly hat. 'You might need this to keep your ears warm.'

He tried to put it over his bizarrely swept back hair, leaving tufts hanging down the back and flopping over his eyes.

'Very cute,' Grace said, unlocking the front door.

Smiling like a child with some new toys, the strange man bounded out of the condo and down the steps to the sidewalk as if he had never been fitter. Seconds later, his voice floated up from the opposite side of the road.

'Which way, Grace? Left or right?'

'Left, to the park. But wait for me.' She knew however that he would be gone, and sure enough it took her a good five minutes to locate him in the park.

He was seated on a small bench, staring at a pond. The woolly hat now lay beside him.

He did not look up as she approached, but simply threw a small pebble into the pond, watching intently as the ripples spread out to the edges.

'Just who am I, Grace?' he said.

'I don't know,' she replied. 'Maybe you're the result of some weird genetic experiment?'

'I don't think so.' He stared out at the water, his chin resting on his hands.

'Well,' Grace tried a different tack. 'Do you have any recollection of your family?'

'No, I —' He suddenly sat upright. 'No, wait. There is something. I remember . . . my father?' He stood up, eyes suddenly bright again. 'Yes, I remember my father. I remember lying back in the grass with my father on a warm Gallifreyan night.' He paused. 'The sky was burnt orange, rich and beautiful and the moonlight made all the leaves glow silver. We lived on the south side of Gallifrey, near a mountain.' He looked Grace straight in the eye, smiling. 'It was covered with the most beautiful daisies.'

Grace nodded. 'This Gallifrey. Somewhere in Ireland perhaps? It sounds Celtic. Scotland?' She remembered the man who had died, the man whose body had had the micro-probe lost inside it. The man whose body had disappeared, only to be apparently replaced by this completely different, but very alive person before her. Could it all be true?

'What else do you remember?'

The man smiled, as if these most important memories were so vivid, so real to him. 'There was a meteor shower that night. The sky was dancing with lights. Purple, green, brilliant yellow.'

He sighed. 'Yes, perfect.'

'What is?'

The man suddenly threw his arms into the air and twirled around, grinning happily. He stopped and bent over slightly, staring right into Grace's face. 'These shoes. They fit perfectly. Thank you.'

Chang Lee had never seen so many books, not even in the Jasmine Library, where he and Pik Sim had hidden from one of the gangs once.

The Master had led him over to the books and, after rummaging around in a cupboard on the opposite side of the room, had found a set of library steps on wheels. He pressed a stud on the bottom of the steps and rung after rung materialised on top. Chang Lee could not see where the top shelf was, but assumed that there were potentially enough rungs to reach it.

The Master was now about eighteen shelves up, searching for something. Chang Lee glanced-surreptitiously over at he main double doors that led back towards Rose Alley, but decided to stick with the Master for now. He seemed a bit weird, but okay enough.

Most importantly, despite the fact that Chang Lee heard him talking to himself a couple of times, the Master had not tried to hurt him, which was unusual enough in itself. Chang Lee was not given to trusting people, but somehow the Master made him feel relaxed and confident. All Chang Lee had to do was help him get his body back from this guy who had stolen it.

The Master pointed up towards the uppermost books and swung his arm around the whole place. 'All this was mine, Chang Lee. Mine until he stole it from me.'

He looked back at Chang Lee. 'He should never have been here. He's changed things, moved my belongings about.'

'You know, I was told he was dead.'

The Master nodded. 'Oh, yes, that body was dead, but now he's regenerated into another. My body can do this twelve times, but he has stolen most of the regenerations.'

Chang Lee was having a job following this. 'What did he do with them exactly?'

'Unspeakable crimes.'

'Like what?'

'Ghengis Khan,' the Master said, climbing back down. Clearly he was annoyed at not having found what he had been searching for.

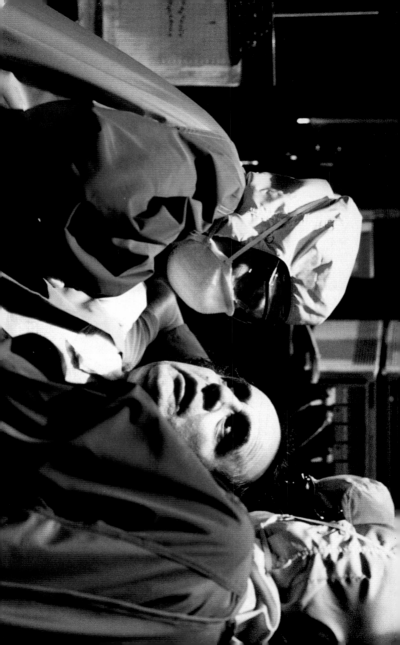

Chang Lee could not quite follow this chain of thought either. The Master had a habit of going off at tangents. 'What about Ghengis Khan?'

'That was him.'

'No way!'

'Oh, yes.' The Master shrugged. 'I'm no saint, rest assured my young friend. But he is totally evil.'

The Master hurried over to another wall – which seemed to be row upon row of filing cabinets. He dragged the steps over with him and climbed up again. 'I was on the verge of finally stopping him when we arrived and –' He stopped suddenly. 'Where would something as valuable as –' He clicked his fingers. 'Of course.' He stared a bit longer, then pulled open the drawer for G. 'There they are.'

He descended slightly and beckoned for Chang Lee to climb the bottom few steps. 'What do you want out of your life, my friend?'

'What d'you mean?'

The Master smiled, and even through the shades, Chang Lee could see the green eyes glowing a bit brighter than before. 'If you could have anything, anything at all in the universe, what would it be?'

Chang Lee thought about this. One thing he had learned after a few years of dealing with guns and drugs, triads and gangs was that the safest, most comfortable people were those with lots of money. A never-ending supply of cash. 'I don't know,' he began, hoping that the Master would be taken in by his indecision, and not think him greedy. 'A million dollars?'

The Master laughed. 'Only a million? How petty. How typically small minded of you humans. A million dollars!'

'Okay,' said Chang Lee, realising he had misjudged this bit. 'Two million.'

'Oh, think bigger, boy.'

'A billion.'

The Master nodded. 'Exactly. And what would you do with a billion dollars? What would you buy?'

Chang Lee had no hesitation there. 'Power.'

The Master smiled. 'Excellent. And it could be yours so easily.'

Chang Lee was now very interested indeed. This was really working out well. 'How?'

The Master reached inside the drawer and brought out a tiny little leather bag. He tossed it to Chang Lee, who caught it easily, and tugged on the tiny binding. The bag opened, revealing what looked like sand.

Then Chang Lee looked harder, and realised it was glittering in the light.

'Gold? Gold dust?'

The Master closed the drawer and jumped off the steps, kicking them backwards.

Chang Lee realised that the Master was deliberately trying to stop him from making a note of which level the right drawer was on. No big deal; years on the streets had made Chang Lee an expert at mapping things out in his mind. He took in various scratches on the cabinet and the position of the drawers both opposite and below certain scuffed steps. No, finding this hidden cache would be no problem in the future. But for now, he would help the Master. While it suited him.

'You get the rest,' the Master was saying, 'when I get my proper body back. A deal?'

Chang Lee pocketed the bag and shook the Master's hand, nodding. 'Deal.'

The Master led the way out of the console room and down a vast corridor. Chang Lee had long since given up trying to work out how this place, this TARDIS, could be so infinitely large. He had walked around the outside. The police had walked around the outside. People from the DA's office had probably walked around the outside; so how come it seemed to be about four foot square outside and, so far, twice the size of Chinatown inside?

He did not have a clue what 'dimensionally transcendental' meant, but the Master had seem convinced that phrase explained it all and Chang Lee thought it wise not to push the point further. Anyway, the Master had seemed quite happy to hand out gold dust, and all he wanted was Chang

Lee's help in capturing this nasty piece of work who had usurped his body. Once the Master had his true body back, Chang Lee would be rich enough to run the triads, the gangs and most of San Francisco.

What to do with all that money, though? Half of him wanted to take over everyone, make them work for him. But something at the back of his mind remembered all his father's comments about wealth corrupting people without them realising it. If spent wisely, money could make you happy, but could also make others happy. Which was best: to buy people's happiness or earn it?

This was something he'd think about later, once he'd got his billion dollars.

The Master stopped suddenly, pointing at a huge set of wooden double doors. He pushed against them, with little success.

'Can you open these, Chang Lee?'

Chang Lee doubted he could. The Master, in Bruce's body, was over six feet tall and quite muscular. If the Master could not shift the doors, he doubted that he, at five foot eight and wiry, had a chance. Nevertheless, he tried. He reached out to touch the doors with one hand. His fingers merely brushed the crack, when the doors shot open inwards with alarming speed.

Chang Lee jumped back, amazed and momentarily frightened. 'How did I do that?'

The Master smiled, his eyes glowing brightly once again behind Bruce's dark shades. 'I told you – the TARDIS really likes you. Come on in, this is my favourite part of the ship.'

As soon as Chang Lee entered the new area, he felt a smile inch across his face. The air was clean, fresh and slightly breezy. There was a wonderful feeling of . . . well, calm about the place. He could not remember feeling this relaxed for ages. Ever since the events of the previous night, he had been running on empty, pushing himself to keep going.

Here, he just felt as if something had washed all those problems, fears and tiredness away.

The word that leaped unbidden into his mind was one he remembered his mother using once, to describe a quiet Sunday afternoon after eating a family lunch.

Serene.

Chang Lee was standing in a massive stone square, uneven paving slabs all over the ground. Small weeds and shrubs sprouted up through the cracks and a few autumnal leaves were swept over the ground by the slight wind. Surrounding the square were pillared walkways, and the Master was hurrying off towards one of them. The whole place reminded Chang Lee of pictures he'd seen of British universities, like Oxford and that other place, Cambridge. He looked up, but in place of the bright light that typified the rest of the

TARDIS, there actually seemed to be a blue sky miles up, with tiny white clouds drifting across it.

He knew that it was impossible, but this place really made him feel as if he was in the open air.

Still smiling, he ran after the Master, catching up with him a moment or two later by one of the pillared walkways.

'What we want is down here, my young friend.'

The Master pointed along the walkway, along more paving stones, between the double columns of pillars.

'This place is awesome,' Chang Lee finally said.

The Master nodded. 'The Cloisters.'

Faintly, as if far away and carried by the wind, Chang Lee could hear a bell pealing. Like a church bell, sombre and slightly doom-laden. He turned, trying to see if he could see a church, or some other building, but the horizon just melted away, like the haze of a mirage and he found it impossible to judge the distances in the Cloisters. All he could see were paved areas, trees and shrubs.

The Master tapped him on the shoulder. 'Through here.'

Chang Lee followed his mentor, ducking under an ivy-wrapped pergola, around some trellises draped with honeysuckle and into a grassed square, tiny daisies dotted over it.

In the centre of the square was a huge building, like a massive church or, what were they called? Cathedrals. Yes, this was big enough to be a cathedral. The Master had gone inside and so Chang Lee followed.

He found himself in a fantastically huge room, with stained-glass windows all round, carved wooden floors and on the far side a massive flight of wooden steps leading upwards. At the top it separated into two balconies, going right and left, which encircled the whole structure, meeting above the doorway through which they had entered. Flaming torches flickered, giving the air a slightly foggy look. The face of an old man with a long beard was carved into the intricate lattice work that decorated the woodwork both above and below the balcony and all over the walls behind it.

In the centre of this, lying flat, was an ornate sculpture, carved from solid granite.

It was an eye; closed, but very definitely an eye. It rested on a rectangular plinth and looked straight upwards. At each corner of the plinth was a much smaller eye, these ones open. Rising straight up from the centre of each eye was a six foot ornate sceptre. Near the top of each sceptre was a round mirror, curved slightly inwards, towards the major eye in the centre. The mirrors were reflecting tiny beams of multi-coloured light from each other in a criss-cross pattern across the eye, almost as if they were protecting it. Every so often, a light beam would miss the opposing mirror and shoot off into the distance, replaced immediately by another. Chang Lee reasoned that although not noticeable, the mirrors had to be moving fractionally all the time to enable this to happen.

It was quite the most beautiful thing he had ever seen.

'What is it?'

The Master smiled. 'It is known as the Eye of Harmony, named after a massive power source back at my home. It powers the TARDIS and everything in it. These beams of Artron energy are what keep everything flowing smoothly, and the Eye is keyed to the biorhythms of both the ship and its . . . its operator.'

Chang Lee pointed to the face which, he noticed, was also carved into the base of the Eye, along with a swirling figure of eight-like symbol.

'Who's Grandad?'

'Ah,' the Master smiled. 'My mentor. The fore-father of all Time Lords and my greatest hero. That is Rassilon, without whom none of us would be here. That symbol is the Great Seal of Rassilon. Wherever you see it, you know you are in a place of great power.'

Change Lee was almost stupefied by the array

of lights; the complexity and beauty of it all. 'And how can this Eye of Harmony help us find your enemy?'

The Master looked towards the Eye of Harmony, running a hand along one of the mirror-supporting sceptres. 'The Eye used to belong to me. Now it is used by him, so if we can open it, we'll find him. It will literally show us where he is.'

'Cool.' Chang Lee walked over and looked down at one corner of the eye. 'So, are you going to open it?'

'Alas, I can't. He has seen to that. But you seem able to operate the TARDIS quite well. Why don't you see if you can pull out one of these mirrored sceptres.' The Master tapped the one he had been holding.

Chang Lee walked towards it. 'Just like that?'

'Just like that.'

With a shrug, Chang Lee flexed his fingers, and then gripped the sceptre. Expecting some resistance, he began heaving, only to discover it slipped up and out of its mooring with ease. Carefully he laid the sceptre on the wooden floor, making sure the mirror did not get damaged.

From the hole in the open eye, a thick beam of light, presumably this Artron energy the Master talked about, shot up, disappearing into the wooden arched ceiling a long way above.

The Master was at his shoulder, speaking quietly. 'It cannot possibly harm you, Chang Lee. It is just light. It is neither hot nor cold; it will not injure you in any way.'

Chang Lee frowned. 'So?'

'Look straight into the light. Right up close. If the TARDIS really likes you, as I suspect it does, the Eye of Harmony will open. For you alone.'

'You keep talking as if this TARDIS of yours is alive. As if it thinks. Can it really be helping me?'

The Master smiled. 'The TARDIS is not alive in any way you can comprehend. Its circuitry, its power and mechanics are far more advanced than your mind could begin to understand. It reacts more in an empathic way; it is guided and motivated by sensing your feelings.'

The Master took him by the shoulders. 'You are a very pleasant young man. Very trustworthy. Decent. Therefore it senses it and responds to it. Does that help?'

Chang Lee shrugged. 'Well, I guess so . . .'

'Good.' The Master's smile vanished. 'So, look into the light and open the Eye.'

'Why don't you?'

With a sigh, the Master put an arm around Chang Lee's shoulder. 'My young friend, you saw that I couldn't move the staff. My foe has, in effect, turned my own home against me. But you? You took the staff out with ease.'

He stood back again. 'Go on, give it a try. For me.'

Chang Lee decided that he would. What harm could it do? And this TARDIS thing certainly did seem to like him, so maybe the Master was right.

And then there was all that gold dust as well . . . It was not really any contest.

He walked towards the pillar of light and stared at it, letting his face get closer and closer. He felt a slight breeze on his face and could smell . . . something nice. Jasmine. Herbs.

It smelled like his parents' house, back in the good old days. It was a wonderful smell, and he smiled.

Beside him, the Eye of Harmony began to open.

He was dimly aware of the Master's voice, penetrating through the rush of the light noise. 'Who do you see, boy? What can you see?'

Chang Lee tried to concentrate, but all he could focus on was a peculiar sound, soft and resonant. He realised it sounded like singing; like the songs his mother used to sing to him when he was really young. Not lullabies, but ancient Chinese songs; tales of bravery and virtue as ancient princes and princesses fought off evil dark lords and wizards. Something was nagging at him, as if this was trying to tell him something, pass a message on.

'Concentrate, boy. What is there?'

Chang Lee closed his eyes for a second and

then reopened them. The singing was fainter now and he could see space. Stars and planets, comets shooting through. It was as if he was seeing the whole universe in one tiny area. He felt he could reach out, touch the stars, learn so many truths about everything. And himself.

At the centre of this universe, the stars began to distort, to move, forming a shape. Gradually, other stars and planets began to fill in the gaps until this shape solidified.

It was a face. A man's face. It was dark and indistinct. Gradually another, then another face appeared until there were six of them, cloudy and unclear, fluctuating slightly.

Chang Lee realised with shock what he was seeing as the seventh face appeared. He recognised the small, puckish features with their soulful eyes and toothy grin as belonging to the man shot outside the TARDIS the night before. These were all the bodies the Master's enemy had appropriated before, and perhaps, like the unfortunate Master, they had rightfully been someone else's. This evil man appeared to be some sort of physical vampire, stealing other people's lives and living them until it was time to move on.

'That's the guy from last night. The one you – the one Bruce – took to the hospital.'

'The Doctor's past lives.'

'The Doctor?'

'That is what he calls himself. He has a brilliant mind, but uses it only for evil.' The Master urged Chang Lee on. 'Can you see what he looks like now?'

Chang Lee watched as the strange man from the previous night dissolved and was replaced by a slightly younger, longer faced man. However, the beaky nose was back and the shape of the eyes and mouth were similar. He had lots of back hair, sticking up and out. This new face possessed piercing pale blue eyes and something of a frown.

The face expanded outward, getting larger and larger. In alarm, Chang Lee stepped away from the Artron energy, expecting the face to vanish, but it was all around him. The sky, the horizon, the ground. He and the Master were standing next to the Eye of Harmony but hovering on a huge image of the Doctor's latest face.

Chang Lee looked over to the Master, who was examining the Doctor's face in minute detail. 'The eyes,' he muttered. 'I can see the retinal pattern.'

He suddenly laughed. 'Of course, that explains so much. His obsession with this dreary planet especially.'

He swung round to Chang Lee, his dark glasses gone, bearing down on the Chinese boy with green serpentine eyes. 'Did you know, the Doctor once boasted of being "more than *just* a Time Lord"?'

Chang Lee was bewildered now – this was getting slightly out of his league. 'Oh, yeah, right. What?'

'He really should have said "*less* than just a Time Lord"! He's half-human – a hybrid. A mongrel!' He let out a huge peal of laughter. 'Oh, Doctor, I have finally discovered your dirty secret. And your weakness.'

This was all getting too much for Grace. The strange man had been lying flat on his back, staring upwards and shaking violently.

Grace had dealt with seizures during her training, but this seemed different. He had not done anything other than suddenly collapse without warning. There had been no cry, no exclamation. One moment he had been staring at the trees, the next he went down, like a puppet whose strings had been cut.

She had been at his side in seconds, waving away a young couple that were walking their dog. Although they had offered to help, they had kept their distance. 'It's all right, I'm . . . I'm his doctor,' Grace had said. As was normal in modern America, the young couple had not really wanted to get involved and with a look of relief, hurried away.

'What is it?' Grace had asked him.

'Something's happening,' he had gasped

through clenched teeth. 'In my . . . my TARDIS! He's in my TARDIS!'

'In your *what*?'

Then he had sat bolt upright, a huge smile across his face. 'Yes!' he cried. 'Yes, I remember everything.'

Now here he was, running about the park, euphoric and full of energy. He ran towards her and suddenly stopped, smiling infectiously.

Grace smiled back.

'I know who I am,' he said simply. He hugged Grace tightly, kissing her full on the lips, passionately. Then he pulled back, embarrassment on his face. 'I'm sorry, I got carried away!'

Grace shrugged. 'Well, fine. Whatever.' Then she looked at him, encouragingly. 'Well, who are you then?'

'I'm the Doctor.' He grinned. 'I am the Doctor.' He suddenly shouted up at the night sky. 'I am the Doctor!'

'Great,' said Grace, pulling him closer. 'Now. Kiss me again!'

He struggled free. 'No. No, I'm sorry. No time.'

Grace felt . . . well, she was not sure. Bewildered, certainly. And not just by him. Here she was, normally calm and rational. Here he was, with two hearts, inhuman blood and the ability to molecularly alter his physiognomy (apparently) and she wanted to kiss him. Why? She did not even know his name until ten seconds ago. The Doctor? That was not a name, it was a description. It might explain how he was able to think clearly about his weird body, but he was like no other doctor she'd ever seen.

'All right, Doctor, what is –'

He cut her off by putting his fingers to her lips. 'I saw him, well, felt him really, in the TARDIS. The Master. He must have found a human body to inhabit, which means it won't last for long. The morphant can't keep a host going for long.' He suddenly slapped his forehead, rather over-dramatically. 'Of course, he's after me.' He grabbed Grace's shoulders, not roughly, but certainly in agitation. 'Don't you understand, Grace? He wants my body. He's going to take it so he can live and I will die!'

Then he stopped, crunching his eyes shut. 'No!'

'What now?'

'He's using the Eye of Harmony, to see through my eyes. I mustn't let him see you.'

Grace was getting more and more bewildered. Almost panicking, but she did not really know why. 'What's the Eye of Harmony?'

In the cathedral-like room, by the Eye of Harmony, the Master and Chang Lee watched as the Doctor's face distorted, changing to a woman's face.

'At last,' the Master whispered. 'We're seeing

112

through the Doctor's eyes. We can see where he is exactly.'

Chang Lee frowned. 'I know that face . . . It's the doctor from the hospital. The one I got the Doctor's bag from.'

The face was frowning, speaking. Concentrating, Chang Lee realised he could hear her words, seeing and listening as he was from the Doctor's point of view.

The image whited out, leaving nothing but stars, planets and comets. The universe as Chang Lee had seen it earlier. The Doctor had closed his eyes, Chang Lee guessed, but he could still hear their words.

'What's going on, Doctor?' the woman from the hospital demanded.

'The Eye of Harmony, it's the power source at the very heart of the TARDIS.'

Chang Lee could hear as the woman took a deep breath. 'Okay. Now then, what is a TARDIS?'

'The TARDIS is my spaceship. It carries me through time and space. T-A-R-D-I-S, an acronym for Time And Relative Dimension In Space.'

Chang Lee was finding this almost as bizarre as he guessed the doctor from the hospital must find it.

'And this "Master",' she was saying. 'Is he like, the Devil?'

'No,' said the Doctor. 'He's a rival Time Lord.'

'A Time Lord.' The woman then spoke quietly. 'Oh my God, you're completely insane.'

'No, I'm not. The Master is pure evil. I was taking his remains home to Gallifrey. In his final incarnation he had been captured by the Daleks, placed on trial and exterminated.'

'And these Daleks? Are they Time Lords, too? Do they have spaceships like your TARDIS?' The sarcasm was obvious.

The Doctor was ignoring her. 'But he wasn't dead. It's all been a trap. A trap for me! He wants me to look into the Eye.'

'So?'

'So, if I look into the Eye of Harmony, my soul will be destroyed. He will be free to take my body then.'

'Listen to all those lies, my young friend.' The Master was beside Chang Lee, hissing into his ear. 'Can you believe this rubbish?'

'No.' Chang Lee was certain. 'But how can she fall for it?'

'Because,' the Master replied, 'he is pure evil. He is exerting his evil force over her. Manipulating all her thoughts and actions. Poor woman.'

'Look,' the doctor from the hospital was saying, her voice echoing around the starscape that Chang Lee was gazing intently at. 'I'm afraid I really can't deal with this.'

'Please, Grace. Listen carefully –'

'No,' the woman, Grace apparently, shouted. 'No. I've had enough.'

'If the Eye of Harmony remains open for too long, this planet will be sucked through it.' The Doctor was sounding desperate.

Chang Lee could hear why. What a load of rubbish.

The Doctor was still shouting at Grace. 'I must fix the timing mechanism on the TARDIS so that I can close the Eye of Harmony. I need an atomic clock. Can you help me find one?'

There was no reply. 'Grace?'

The image of the park suddenly burst back into the cathedral as the Doctor presumably opened his eyes. Chang Lee could see Grace running across the park.

'So, that's how he intends to destroy me.'

The Master looked across to Chang Lee. 'We must find the Doctor before he finds an atomic clock.'

Chang Lee was staring at the image of Grace running away from the Doctor. The movement of the image suggested that the Doctor was following. He pointed at Grace. 'Yeah, she's the woman at the hospital all right. Bet Bruce would have some way of finding out where she lives.'

'Excellent suggestion, my friend. If we find her, we find him.'

The Master turned and clicked his fingers at Chang Lee, indicating that he should follow him.

As he left the Eye of Harmony, Chang Lee looked back, but without their presence everything had reverted to just the cathedral.

The Doctor had reached the steps outside Grace's apartment. He could hear her locking the door to keep him out.

'Grace!'

With a despairing shake of his head, he ran up the steps, taking all four in one go, his alien body powered with slightly better agility and energy than a human's. One of Grace's neighbours, an old lady with a cat in her arms, cowered back into the porch of her own front door as he stood outside Grace's, trying to see in somehow.

'Good evening.' He stopped, and tugged at the front of his hairline in an old fashioned greeting. 'I'm awfully sorry about this disturbance. Have a happy New Year.'

With a cheerful smile he continued yelling at Grace.

Grace was breathing deeply, half catching her breath, half trying to relax. Maybe Roger Swift had been right – she should have ignored all this weirdness and got on with her job. She'd call him later, apologise and see if she could get her job back. She needed some normality, no matter how dreary, after the totally bizarre events of today.

She was beginning to convince herself everything was going to be all right when there was a frantic hammering on the door, interspersed with a very English shout of 'Grace!' every so often.

She could not ignore it; even if she tried, the neighbours would complain. Mrs Trattorio would claim her cat was being unfairly disturbed, or some kind of rubbish like that.

'Go away, Doctor,' was all she could think to shout back. 'Stay away from me.'

'Grace,' came the pleading reply. 'Just let me in.'

'No!'

There was a pause, and Grace moved closer to the phone. An idea was coming, a way she could be rid of this weirdo she'd encouraged by kissing him. How stupid could she be; kissing a man before finding out he thought he was from another planet. Good move, Grace.

'Grace,' he started again. 'Grace, if you let me in, we can calm down, have a cup of tea, and talk about this. Reasonably.'

'Sure,' Grace yelled back. '"Earth calling Time Lord. Earth to Time Lord."'

There was a pause. Grace thought he'd actually given up. She moved nearer the phone, grabbing her address book from out of her bag. She had just reached the phone when he started again.

'You're right, Grace.'

Success?

'I am a Time Lord.'

Failure.

She sat down, and called back over her shoulder towards the door. 'And I thought you were a doctor.'

'And I thought *you* were a doctor,' came the retort.

She made a decision, and began punching numbers on the phone. 'Listen,' she said. 'I'm going to call for an ambulance to take you back to the psychiatric ward from which you obviously escaped.'

Outside in the porch, the Doctor was kneeling, trying to see through the keyhole. Gradually he became aware that someone was watching him. Slowly he turned, smiling benignly at the old lady with the cat.

'Lover's tiff,' he said, hoping that would suffice.

'Makes a change from the other one, I s'pose,' she said. Then she glanced down at the Doctor's feet. 'Shoes,' she said simply.

'Yes, shoes,' he agreed.

'They're the other one's shoes. You didn't last long then. He only moved out last night.'

The Doctor smiled. 'Really? That's very interesting, but actually I'm trying to convince Dr

Holloway to let me in. If ever I see Brian, I'll return his shoes.'

'Bad luck, walking around in other people's shoes,' the elderly neighbour grunted. As if to reinforce the point, her cat jumped down from her arms, hissed at the Doctor and shot away, presumably to its own door. The elderly lady gave him a last malicious look and followed her pet.

The Doctor turned back to the keyhole, but could not see a thing through it. 'Grace, we really don't have time for this. The Eye of Harmony is open and if I don't get to my TARDIS and close it, this planet will no longer exist. I doubt the Master even knows what he's doing.' Or even cares, he thought, but decided not to impart that idea to Grace. 'I reckon we've got till about midnight. Not long.'

'Shut up,' came the reply from inside the condo. 'I'm getting an ambulance for you.'

The Doctor realised he was not getting anywhere. He needed to make her see sense. He reached down to where his fob-watch used to be, but it was with his other things . . . somewhere.

He tried the doorhandle and then stared at it. Where he had gripped it, his fingers had made severe indentations. He knew he was not quite that strong and there had to be another explanation.

Of course . . .

He looked along the front of the apartment. A set of french windows overlooked the street and he hurried towards them. He could now see Grace inside, her back to him, indeed on the telephone.

'Yes, I'll hold,' he heard her say. Then, while waiting, she saw something on the coffee table opposite and reached out for it. The Doctor tried to see, but it was dark outside and Grace only had a lamp on rather than an overhead light.

Then he saw it caught in the glow. It was the microsurgical probe he had tugged out of his chest earlier. Instinctively he reached for his wound, but it had healed up.

Beside the probe were papers; probably the notes she had made about his blood type, pulse rate and other cardio-vascular measurements that would be more than slightly unusual if he were a human. She simply had to accept he was right.

He tapped on the french windows and felt a twinge of remorse as Grace jumped with fright. He could see that it was more than that – she was actually frightened of him.

Just what must he represent to her?

A weirdo, as she shouted earlier? Or a true alien? As a doctor, surely, she had to accept that scientifically, the Doctor was not as he seemed and therefore his explanation of being from another world had to be plausible, if not logical. What else could he do to prove it to her?

'Grace,' he shouted through the glass, 'I'm going to prove to you that the Eye of Harmony is open. Look at this!'

He pressed his hand against her french windows. And pushed. The glass stretched under the pressure, like polythene, going further and further into the room. Eventually his hand went through it, without breaking the glass. With a monumental effort he pushed his shoulder and eventually his whole body through, and was standing in her living room. The glass snapped back into place, and they both turned to stare at it; unbroken and unmarked, as if nothing had happened.

'You see,' he said. 'Already the molecular structure of the planet is changing. At first in subtle ways, like that, but soon it'll be catastrophic.'

Trying not to be distracted by her gaping at the window, he circled around her, trying to draw her attention away from the phone still pressed to her ear. 'By midnight tonight, this whole planet will be pulled inside-out. There will be nothing left. No humans, no animals. No trees, no flowers. No air, no water. Nothing, Grace.' He sat down. 'Nothing to show your race ever even existed. Not even Darjeeling tea, mom's apple pie or Hershey bars.'

Grace finally looked at him, and spoke into her phone. 'Yes, this is Dr Holloway. I need an ambulance at my home right away. I need a bed in the psychiatric ward.'

She stared hard at the Doctor, as if trying to take in everything he said, despite her astonishment at what she had seen happen to the window.

'Better make that two beds,' she said and put the phone down.

Joey Sneller was worried. He'd been at work since midday, when his shift had started but there had been no sign of Bruce, his paramedic partner.

Today it was Bruce's turn to drive, and yet he had simply vanished. Shelly Curtis had said she'd seen him that morning, acting weirdly, and guessed that Miranda had thrown a tantrum. But Joey thought it unlikely. He had called Bruce's apartment but got a recorded message from Miranda, saying they were unable to reach the phone and to call back later. Joey had done this four times now. Old man Prentiss had been worried too – Bruce was renowned for both his reliability and punctuality. This bizarre disappearance was extremely out of character.

As Bruce was not around, two other paramedics had rearranged their shifts to cover. The first had gone home about twenty minutes ago, and the other was apparently on his way over from St Genesius, right across town. Joey just hoped he wasn't called out on an emergency before the new guy got there.

A scuffle behind him made him look out of the

ambulance cabin, and a grin spread across his face. 'Bruce, my man, where've you been? We were really worried.'

'I'm very sorry.'

Joey stared hard at Bruce. They'd been friends and colleagues for some years now, and there was something wrong. It was not just the fact that Bruce was wearing shades at night, it was something in the way he . . . he walked oddly. Kind of jerkily, as if he was wearing shoes too small for him, or something.

Bruce's face came right up to the wound-down window, just as their two-way radio crackled, ordering them to Dr Holloway's apartment.

'Get the address,' Bruce snapped.

'Okay, man,' said Joey. 'I thought you knew all the staff's home addresses.'

'Shut up and get the address!'

Joey knew then that something was very wrong. Perhaps Bruce had been drinking. He got the address off the radio operator but kept his hands on the ambulance keys. 'I think I'd best drive, Bruce,' he said.

Bruce suddenly opened the cab door, which Joey thought was a rather aggressive action, something else out of character.

He was still thinking that when Bruce smacked a flattened hand against the side of his neck, shattering it.

* * *

The Master hauled the corpse out of the driving seat and dragged it to the other side of a nearby parked car, dumping it there.

Wiping his hands, he crossed back to the ambulance and started it up. He reversed out of the hospital and down towards the main street.

Chang Lee was waiting on the corner. He had been reluctant to return to the hospital in case anyone recognised him.

'Any problems?' he asked, climbing aboard.

The Master smiled. 'None. No one was around.' He repeated Grace's address, asking if Chang Lee knew where it was.

The boy nodded and began giving instructions. 'It's near the Bay Area,' he said.

The Master drove on. *Not long now, Doctor,* he thought. *Soon your body will be mine.*

The Doctor marched out of the bathroom.

'I've lost twenty pounds,' he said.

Grace tried to smile benignly. Treat him nicely, keep him calm, and the ambulance should be here soon. Just keep him chatting until then. 'Congratulations,' she smiled.

'In twenty minutes.'

'Well, look on the bright side.' She was waiting to hear footsteps in the hallway outside. What was taking them so long? 'You could make a fortune in the weight loss business.'

The Doctor sat in front of the television, grabbing the remote off the table. 'I'm serious. It's starting.' He began channel hopping. 'News,' he muttered. 'Which is the news?'

'Try KKBE,' Grace said helpfully. 'Channel 7.'

The Doctor nodded. 'Good idea.' He pressed the correct button and the face of a young, dark-haired Japanese newsreader popped up.

'This is KKBE, broadcasting to San Francisco, and I'm Mi-Jung Kanaka. And now for more on that item we trailed earlier.' A photograph of the Golden Gate Bridge appeared behind her. 'Some people are calling it "The Millennium Effect". Since earlier this evening, Bay Area tides have risen to levels that break all records for this time of year. Flood warnings have gone out along the Napa and Russian Rivers, and this just in . . .' The picture changed to show a man in a loud shirt and shorts sitting in thick snow, grinning. 'Hawaii is experiencing snowdrifts!'

The Doctor caught Grace's eye. 'What will it take, Grace, to prove to you I'm telling the truth?'

The KKBE anchorwoman continued. 'Now, maybe you're wondering what this has to do with tonight's millennium? Well, we've been told that these freak conditions are due to very slight fluctuations in Earth's gravitational pull. Fluctuations that apparently only happen every thousand years. We go over to Sean Ley in San Jose where some people are claiming it has been raining fish!'

The Doctor was laughing humourlessly. 'I love you humans. So parochial in your views. If it doesn't fit the facts, change the facts. You see patterns in things that aren't there.'

Grace was going to reply when she heard voices outside. Mrs Trattorio, and it sounded as if she was pointing someone in Grace's direction.

The Doctor was still engrossed in the KKBE news, so Grace slipped over towards the door. She hoped they had good straps on the stretcher, because she doubted the Doctor would go easily.

'And when we come back,' said the woman on television, 'we'll be showing you where the wealthiest and most fashionable San Franciscans are going tonight to see in the millennium.'

The shot cut to a tall, blonde co-anchor, standing in front of a massive local map, dotted with icons for rain, snow, hail and lightning. 'Didn't I hear that they're all off to see a clock being started?'

It cut back to the anchorwoman, smiling. The Doctor leaned forward, turning up the volume so loudly he did not hear the knock at the door. Grace opened it, putting her fingers over her lips. She was overjoyed to see it was Bruce, but there was no sign of Joey. She pointed to the sofa, where the Doctor's back was clearly visible. Bruce nodded, understandingly.

'It's not just any old clock, Joanna. This is apparently the most accurate atomic clock in the world. And yes, it's right here, in good old down-town San Francisco, at our very own Institute of Technological Advancement and Research. Now, don't go away because –'

The Doctor flicked the switch off, and jumped up to see Grace talking to a man with car keys in his hand.

'They're here, Doctor –' began Grace as the Doctor ran over.

'Excellent. They can take us straight to the Institute.' He looked at Bruce. 'Do you know where that is?'

Bruce shot Grace a look and she just nodded, hoping he'd get the message. Humour him, he's completely gone.

'Of course I do,' Bruce said.

Grace finally allowed herself to smile as she threw a jacket over her shoulders.

'Thanks, Bruce,' she said. 'Nice shades.'

Bruce just smiled again. 'No problem, Grace. Believe me, this is no problem.'

Four for a boy

Fifteen minutes later, Grace decided that she was not enjoying her New Year's Eve in the slightest. She ought to have been at a party, dancing around someone's house, having a good time.

Yeah, definitely a good party, and not racing down the road towards Walker General, in the back of an ambulance with whoever was up front – Joey in all probability – driving as if he'd never driven anything larger than a bicycle. More than once she had muttered to Bruce about it, wondering if Joey had perhaps drunk more than he should. Bruce had shrugged and been quite taciturn, causing Grace to wonder if they'd both had too much office vino that afternoon.

The Doctor was being thankfully quiet, staring out of the rear window, hunched on the end of the stretcher in his ridiculous fancy dress costume, looking like he ought to be celebrating the end of the nineteenth century and not the twentieth.

'What time is it?' he said, looking back at her, a frown embedded in his forehead.

Grace glanced at her watch. 'It's just gone ten.' She smiled, trying to humour him. Not long now and he'd be Roger Swift's responsibility and she could head off to whatever party she could track down. 'And don't worry,' she added, slightly malicioulsy. 'I'm on the Board of Directors at the Institute. They'll listen to me.'

The Doctor turned back to his observation of the way they had come and Bruce frowned.

'Institute?'

Grace whispered back, pointing at the Doctor. 'He thinks we're going to find some sort of clock at the Institute of Technological Advancement and Research.'

Bruce nodded. 'I wondered what he meant back at your place.'

'Help me keep the pretence up, and have a sedative handy. When he sees the hospital, he'll probably go ape.'

The Doctor suddenly swung back to her. 'Grace, if you know the Board, why didn't you tell me you had access to a beryllium atomic clock?'

Grace floundered for a second. Think! 'I was more concerned and shocked by your discovery.'

'Discovery?'

'Yeah, you know, that Eye of . . . Destruction?'

The Doctor nodded, as if that made it all clear. 'Oh, of Harmony,' he corrected.

Got away with that. Just. 'Yes. That and the fact that this planet will be sucked through it at midnight.' She smiled. 'Let's face it, how often does one have a Time Lord in one's living room, Doctor?'

She threw a quick look at Bruce. 'He likes me to call him "Doctor". Freud had a name for it —'

'"Transference",' said the Doctor. 'That's very good, Grace. But I don't think so. Freud would have taken me seriously.'

Damn, he'd seen through her. Oh well, the hospital could not be far away. Mind you, Joey was obviously taking the long route. Carry on with the charade, Grace. 'Freud would have hung up his pipe if he'd met you, Doctor.'

'As a matter of fact, I did meet him once.'

'Well, of course. You are a Time Lord, after all.' Another look at Bruce. She felt as if she needed some support, but he was just staring at the Doctor through his shades. There was something very strange about them, she noted. Something not quite right.

'Sigmund and I got on very well. I gave him lots of pointers about psychoanalysis.'

Grace sighed. 'I suppose you knew Madame Curie, too?'

'Intimately.'

The Doctor settled down to face them, although Grace noted he was staring at Bruce more often than not. Had he seen something strange in his manner, too?

Oh, what did it matter? He was nutty as a fruitcake.

'Did she kiss as good as me?'

Bruce coughed and corrected Grace's English. '"Did she kiss as *well* as me."'

Grace smiled, but then the ambulance suddenly shuddered to a halt. Joey had either hit a red light at the last minute, or just missed a car. She was about to comment on it, when she saw more cars screech to a halt behind them. 'Guess something's blocking the road ahead.'

The Doctor did not take his eyes off Bruce, and as Grace looked back at him, he murmured something about time running out.

'My favourite planet is about to be destroyed and I'm stuck in a traffic jam.'

He suddenly leaned right forward, towards Bruce.

'Do excuse me,' he said, and grabbed the paramedic's shades, yanking them off.

And then it dawned on Grace that she might have made the tiniest of mistakes. That she may have misjudged the Doctor. And that maybe Joey was not driving the ambulance at all, because whatever was sitting beside her was not the Bruce Gerhardt that she knew.

What was sitting beside her had green, reptilian

eyes, that seemed to be glowing; lit by some kind of green fire behind them.

'Bruce? What's wrong with you?'

The Doctor pushed her against the back doors of the ambulance, scrabbling for the door lever. 'He's the Master!'

Grace barely had time to take this in, because Bruce, or the Master, or whatever he was threw his head back as if gargling and then forward again, spitting at her —

And her arm was in front of her face, a reflex action that, she realised later, saved her life. A green globule of something splashed against her wrist, sending burning pain through it. Grace screamed in agony just as the Doctor kicked at the door and jumped out, hauling her out with him.

The Master also leaned forward, grabbing the Doctor's long frock-coat tails, trying to drag him back in.

Grace found herself sprawled on the hood of a car, its driver clearly unable to believe his eyes. She looked back and saw the Doctor grab a tiny portable fire extinguisher, letting it off at point blank range into the Master's face. With a screech, he let go of the Doctor, who jumped down and took Grace's hand.

'Terribly sorry,' he yelled at the bemused car driver and began running through the middle of the traffic, past the ambulance, weaving in and out of the cars, almost dragging Grace along with him.

She pointed forward. 'What were we doing here?' she yelled. They were almost on the Golden Gate Bridge. 'This is nowhere near Walker General!'

'No,' replied the Doctor. 'But I bet it's the right direction for the Institute.'

'Yes. So?'

'So the Master needs to get there to stop me getting that atomic clock.'

They were actually on the bridge now, still diving in and out of the car lanes, moving a great deal faster than the stationary cars stuck in a grid-lock, going nowhere. It seemed as if every car had decided to create a modern symphony of car horns and Grace actually had to cover her ears as she ran, the noise was so loud.

'Some people are going to spend their New Year's Eve here, by the look of it,' the Doctor laughed.

Grace was trying to understand. 'So, Bruce is the Master?'

'Oh I doubt it, Grace. Knowing the Master, your friend Bruce is long since dead. The morphant creature that housed the Master's consciousness probably took over Bruce's corpse. That's why he needs my body – Bruce's won't hold all that Time Lord energy. Plus it's probably decomposing moment by moment.'

Grace stopped suddenly. 'If I pretend I under-stood every word of that, will you promise not to ask me to repeat it?'

The Doctor grinned. 'Promise.'

They both turned in the direction of a police siren. Sure enough, a motorcycle cop was weaving expertly through the traffic, heading towards them.

Moments later he had stopped before them, drumming his fingers on his handlebars. 'Now, just hold on a moment there, sir. Ma'am.' He looked back towards the ambulance, about twenty cars behind. 'I think you ought to go back to your vehicle.'

The Doctor stuffed his hand inside his jacket, presumably to get something, but Grace realised how the cop would see it. Sure enough, his gun was almost out of its holster when she threw her-self between them.

'Stop,' she cried. 'He's . . .' What could she say? Of course. 'He's English.'

Standing slightly out of the Doctor's eyeline, she tapped her temple, trying to suggest he was a bit strange. The cop nodded, slowly replacing his pistol.

The Doctor produced a crumpled and battered straw hat from within his coat. He offered it towards the cop. Grace could see a white paper bag inside it.

'Would you care for a jelly baby, officer?'

'A what?'

'Just take it,' hissed Grace, mouthing a silent 'please' for good effect.

The cop did as he was told, picked out a green one and began munching. The Doctor meanwhile fumbled and dropped his hat, and then deftly caught it, without spilling a single jelly baby.

Grace was about to say something when she realised the Doctor was now holding the cop's gun.

No matter how surprised Grace was, that was nothing to the look the cop gave. He did a double-take at his own empty holster and then back at this mad Englishman with his straggly long hair, antique clothes, straw hat and gun.

Replacing the straw hat inside his jacket, the Doctor put the pistol carefully against his own head. 'Now stand back, officer, or I'll shoot myself.'

The cop moved back two steps. The other drivers stopped their chorus of honks and toots, staring equally bemused at the scenario played out before them.

'Now, don't be foolish, sir.'

The Doctor did not take his eyes off the cop, but it was to Grace that she spoke. 'Are you with me, Grace?'

A series of random thoughts shot through her head. She saw the Doctor — the other Doctor as she now understood, mortally wounded, in the operating theatre. She saw him begging her not to operate. She remembered losing the micro-probe and then him. There was the parking lot, and the new Doctor with the probe oozing out of his chest. The park. The news reports. The Doctor forcing his way through malleable glass. And the Master, in Bruce's body but able to spit venomous acid at her. Her wrist was blistered still, and she touched it, as if reminding herself that this nightmare was, indeed, real.

'We don't stand a chance,' she murmured.

Still not looking at her, the Doctor spoke quietly. 'I came back, Grace. Back to life before your very eyes. I held back death. I can't make your dream come true forever, Grace, but I can make it come true today. What do you say?'

For a tiny second, an image of her mother flashed through Grace's mind. Before the cancer, before the sickness. Before she died. It was an image Grace had not seen before. If she normally thought of her mother, it was always as she had been in the last few, memorable but tragic weeks. This image was far better.

'Give me the gun,' she said.

The Doctor hesitated this time, but only for a few seconds. Then he lowered the pistol and handed it to her, handle first. Without thinking she pointed it at the cop.

'Give him your keys,' she said.

'Now listen, lady,' the cop said. 'Life can deal you bad hands sometimes, but this is no way –'

To Grace's astonishment, there was an yell from the various drivers surrounding them. 'Give them the damned keys!' they chorused.

His shoulders slumped, the cop passed his motorcycle keys to the Doctor.

The Time Lord turned to face Grace, and smiled.

Grace's heart beat a fraction faster as she smiled back. This might not be such a bad way to see in the millennium after all . . .

The Master was sitting in the passenger seat of the ambulance, wiping the remnants of the extinguisher foam from his face. He fumbled as he replaced his dark glasses.

Chang Lee stared hard at him. The Master's skin was red and raw, but worst of all, some of it had begun peeling away, allowing a faint green light to pulse through from inside his head.

'Yes, this body is finally falling apart,' the Master snapped. 'I need my own back from the Doctor. We have to get to him.'

Chang Lee started the engine up, but did not move the vehicle.

'Well,' the Master snapped, 'what are you waiting for?'

Chang Lee pointed ahead, and spoke quietly.

He tried not to look at the greenish skin of his friend. All he could think of was getting him to the Doctor. And little bags of gold dust. 'The road is still blocked. Everyone going to parties, I guess . . .'

The Master grabbed his hand, almost crushing it, and placed it beside a switch on the dashboard. 'This is an ambulance, boy. Use your siren.'

Chang Lee pulled his hand free, and flicked the siren switch. It started up immediately.

'All right!' he shouted. They began to ease forward as various cars managed to find enough room to let them pass.

The Doctor was starting the motorcycle up when they both heard the siren behind them.

Grace raised the pistol, but the Doctor flicked out his arm, knocking it from her and over the side of the bridge, into the river far below.

'That might have been useful,' she said, astonished.

'I hate guns,' he said, somewhat fiercely. 'They go bang and hurt people.'

'It also would have made a good deterrent,' she snapped back.

'D'you know how to use one safely? How to load it, cock it and aim it properly?'

Grace paused, then admitted that she didn't.

'Exactly,' the Doctor said. 'It might have been you who got hurt, and that I could not live with.'

Somehow, that made Grace happy, and she clutched the Doctor tightly as he revved the bike up and sped off across the Golden Gate Bridge, away from the ambulance and the Master.

Her joy soon turned to terror as she realised that the Doctor had about as much road sense as she had gun sense. He ignored every sign that demanded they stop, causing more than a few cars to swerve at junctions to avoid them. Eventually they saw a sign pointing right, to take them out of the Lombard area of the city centre and off towards the ITAR. At the last moment, the Doctor swung the bike right and headed for the Institute.

'It's on the waterfront,' Grace yelled and the Doctor nodded, seeing it in the distance.

Chang Lee saw them swerve right and promptly went the opposite way, much to his passenger's consternation.

'What are you doing, Chang Lee?' the Master growled.

'It's a quicker way,' Chang Lee said.

'It'd better be —' The Master sounded more menacing than ever before and, for the first time, Chang Lee wondered if he was doing the right thing. Then he remembered the gold dust.

'Look,' he said, perhaps a little too sharply, 'this is my area. I know these streets, this town. Just enjoy the ride. Trust me!'

'If we don't catch the Doctor,' the Master said, 'I'm finished.' He looked at Chang Lee, frowning. 'And so, boy, are you!'

Chang Lee deliberately took the next corner too sharply, and smiled inwardly as he heard the Master's head thump against the window.

'Sorry,' he yelled.

The ambulance went up a slight hill and then bounced over the ridge, all wheels coming off the road before crashing down again. Chang Lee grinned – he'd always wanted to do this. Another five or six similar humps were approaching rapidly.

As they went over the next, Chang Lee glanced at the Master, looking decidedly greener than before. 'Don't worry,' he said.

'I'm not worried,' came the reply.

'When I get all that gold,' Chang Lee said, 'do you know what I'm going to do?'

'I'd rather not,' was the Master's reply, spoken through gritted teeth.

Chang Lee laughed at this.

'I'm glad one of us is amused.' The Master placed both hands on the dashboard, trying to steady himself as they literally flew over another hump, then crashed down, sending sparks back the way they had come.

'Hey, cheer up, man,' said Chang Lee. 'You'll get your body back real soon. We're a team, right?'

'Oh, yes,' the Master replied. 'We're "a team".'

His head banged loudly on the roof.

Speeding along the waterfront, Grace could see over the Doctor's shoulder. The Institute was getting nearer and larger, but she could also see another junction ahead, and the lights turned red. She was about to yell this observation out when the Doctor shot straight through it, nearly causing another pile-up.

'Did you see that stop light?' she screamed in his ear.

'Where?' he called back.

'Doctor?'

'Yes, Grace?'

She sighed. 'Unlike you, I only have one life. Could you please remember that?'

Before the Doctor could answer, they were shooting up the driveway towards the Institute, a huge concrete and glass modern set of buildings looking like they'd been built with Lego blocks, connected to each other by tubular walkways about two storeys up.

They passed a hoarding, with the legend: *2000. THE BEGINNING OF SAN FRANCISCO MEAN-TIME.*

They approached the largest building. All the lights were on and the music and hubbub of a big party could be heard, even over the roar of the bike. Grace noted various security people and media vans littered about.

And she saw something else.

'Oh no, Doctor. Look!'

Parked beside one of the KKBE news vans was the Master's ambulance, both doors open wide.

Five for silver

'I always thought hell would be hot, not sub-zero,' Gareth Fitzpatrick said, shivering and wishing he was somewhere else. 'Makes you wonder what heaven is really like.' He dug his chin under the top of his sweater and rubbed the back of his neck, trying to massage some warmth into it.

'Not exactly what I had in mind for tonight,' agreed David Bailey, his friend, as he pulled his jacket tighter around his own neck. 'I expected a glass of champagne, warmth and a drunken conga around the waterfront.'

Gareth shrugged. 'Well, next time, let's not volunteer to work on New Year's Eve.'

The two of them were standing in the doorway of the Institute of Technological Advancement and Research reception area as guest after guest, dressed in the most expensive suits and gowns they could possibly hire, waved their invitations at them.

Both were students who had anticipated getting free invites to the party by offering to work as security guards for the night. Both were wrong.

They had turned up four hours ago in equally expensively hired dinner jackets, saying that they had come to meet a Mr Vyse, who was expecting them to help out with the guests.

Moments later they had been led to a portakabin at one side of the parking lot and shown inside by a man who looked as though he might once have been a boxer. He had been smirking, as if he knew a joke but had no intention of passing it on. The joke, they came to realise, was that their expensive attire had been a waste of time. In the portakabin were two black jackets, two peaked caps (emblazoned with the legend *VYSE SECURITY*) and a pair of dull grey pants and rather thin black roll-neck sweaters.

Realising that they had been hoodwinked, Gareth and Paul had discontentedly changed and emerged a few moments later to be shown to the front door.

'This is the closest you'll get to being inside at midnight,' their smirking guide said. 'Mr Vyse wants you to check everybody's invite. No one, and I mean no one, gets without one. It's one pass per person. Got that?'

Gareth said that they had indeed got it and since then they had been doing as requested.

David nodded as he checked another man's invite and ushered him through to the reception desk inside the lobby.

'You know, this clock thing would be a good target. If any weird political group wanted to make a statement, they needn't look any further, really. San Francisco's newest achievement blown to pieces.'

'Oh, great,' said Gareth, looking about him.

Maybe they should have stayed home and watched the news reports. But they both needed some cash to tide them over until the start of the next semester, and although this was not very much, it would help.

'Ready for your mid-term?' David asked suddenly.

Gareth shrugged again. 'Yeah. I guess. You?'

'No.' David looked at his feet. 'I'm actually not going back to college next year. I'm dropping out.'

Gareth let this sink in. 'You're what? Why?'

David checked three more guests in. 'I guess I realised last term that all this wasn't what I wanted, you know?' He looked straight at Gareth. 'I thought I did, but now I don't.'

'What did your mom say?'

'She freaked. Dad was cool, though. He understood. He said I should do what I wanted to do.'

'Nice dad,' Gareth said. 'Wish mine was that open-minded.' He checked a woman in, pointing her towards the ladies' rest room when she asked. 'I'm majoring in mathematics and that's an end to it as far as he's concerned.'

'What d'you want to do?' David smiled as another guest thanked him as he went into the lobby.

'I don't really know. But I'm worried about tying myself down to one career while I'm only eighteen.'

'Now you know why I got out,' David said.

Gareth was about to speak again, when someone tapped him on the shoulder. It was a short girl, about his age, with black hair cut into a Louise Brooks-style bob. She was smiling, and Gareth thought it was the most radiant smile he'd ever seen.

'Hi,' he said.

'Hi,' she replied. 'I'm Sophie. I'm on lobby duty, at the desk.' She pointed towards it, and Gareth nodded. 'I need to go to the rest room. Could you cover for me? Just for a second?'

'Sure thing,' Gareth nodded. He threw an apologetic look at David and dashed into the warm lobby.

'You're ace,' Sophie said, grabbing her bag off the back of the chair.

'So are you,' Gareth muttered as she hurried off.

David had now begun letting more guests through and Gareth began pointing them towards the main dining area. He was starting to enjoy this at last.

After a few moments, he looked up to see two people facing him. One was a stunning strawberry-blonde, the other a bizarre-looking man. Neither was really dressed for the occasion, but the man was particularly peculiar. He wore a brown coat, grey pants and a hideous paisley vest. His hair looked like it had not been combed for weeks. The woman followed Gareth's gaze, and leaned forward conspiratorially, showing Gareth her invitation.

'He made a mistake and thought it was fancy dress. By the time we realised . . .' She held her hands out as if to say 'what could we do?'.

'Can I see your pass, sir?' Gareth asked the strange man.

The woman stood between them. 'I'm Dr Grace Holloway. And friend.'

Gareth faced a quandary – this was the first time during the evening that someone had come without an invitation. 'I'm sorry,' he said, 'but no one is allowed in without an invite.'

The blonde waved her invite at him. 'I have an invitation. You're looking at it.'

The man leaned towards them. 'Problem, Grace?'

'I'm on the Board, young man. I can assure you that my guest here is essential to tonight's proceedings.' She threw a look at the man. 'Tell him, Doctor.'

'Oh, yes, right. Yes, I'm very important.' The man smiled at Gareth.

'See?' added Dr Holloway. 'He's Dr Beech, from England.'

She pointed towards the door marked *NO ENTRY* that Gareth assumed led up to the stage area. 'They're waiting for him.'

Dr Beech leaned forward and Gareth squirmed slightly in his seat under the scrutiny. 'Don't I know you, young man?'

Gareth shook his head and indicated that they ought to go through. Anything to get rid of them. He watched them mingle with the crowd and tuned back to the next guest only to find the gorgeous Sophie standing there.

'Hi again,' she said. 'Guess it's back to work for me.'

'Yeah. Okay.' Gareth vacated his seat and headed back to the cold outdoors, and what he thought would be a very jealous David Bailey.

'Hey, handsome, what's your name?'

Gareth felt his skin glow. 'Err . . . Gareth. Gareth Fitzpatrick.'

Sophie nodded. 'All right, Gareth Fitzpatrick. Fancy a dance at midnight?'

Gareth realised that now he knew exactly what heaven was.

★ ★ ★

'That's the first time being on the Board of this place has ever been of any real use to me.'

Grace munched on a couple of vol au vents and took a glass of red Gioberti from a passing waiter. 'You should try some of this, Doctor,' she said. 'Tuscany valley wine. I went down to the vineyard once, watched them make the stuff.' She smiled. 'Got on very well with the owner's son, I seem to remember. Wonder what happened to him?'

The Doctor did not answer her. Instead, he was scanning everybody in the dining room and obviously not finding what he wanted. 'He must have found a back way in,' he muttered. 'We need to be back there.' He pointed towards the empty presentation area, a raised dais, cordoned off with red ropes.

Grace nodded. 'All right.' She indicated the grouped television reporters, with their camera crews, huddled near the area. 'If anyone asks, we're with them.'

'There's the clock,' the Doctor said, pointing directly above them.

'It's huge,' breathed Grace, slightly awestruck. 'I mean, just how are you going to get that on the back of the motorcycle?'

'We only need a tiny piece of it. The beryllium chip that moves the microchips that are essentially powered by the atomic particles that —'

'Built the house that Jack couldn't. Yes, all right.' Grace pulled him forward. 'I gather time is not on our side right now.'

'No, but I've always been on hers.' He grinned. 'She owes me.'

Grace decided she did not want to get too existential right now and thought it best to keep them moving. 'Make conversation, Doctor, people are looking at us.' She stopped briefly and spoke loudly. 'So, time travel is possible then, Doctor?'

'Oh, yes,' he answered, exaggerating his accent and making heads turn. 'But only if you have the right equipment.'

Grace saw that they were near a short stairway which led up behind the dais. She glanced up at the clock, encased within a glass box and looking more like a piece of modern art than a timepiece. There was an access-way behind it, presumably where it had been programmed from. The stairs more than likely led towards it.

'And if, like me, you have the right equipment,' the Doctor was telling an short, attractive woman with glasses, 'anything is possible.'

Grace tried to lean back and grab him, but the short woman interrupted. 'Hi, I'm Professor Sullivan, down from Winona. I thought I'd travelled a long way, but you're from England, right?'

'Wrong,' said the Doctor, smiling at her. 'I'm from Gallifrey.'

150

'Ah.' Professor Sullivan shook his hand. 'I've always wanted to go to Ireland. 'If ever I make it, maybe I can look you up.'

The Doctor nodded. 'Of course. But I'm rarely at home.'

Grace tugged on his sleeve.

'And have you met Dr Holloway?' He pulled her towards him instead. 'She's a very good cardiologist. Never lost a patient yet.'

Professor Sullivan shook Grace's hand. Then she looked at Grace's jeans and blouse, her eyes widening as she took in the black jacket. 'Been working late?'

'Oh, yes,' Grace said through gritted teeth. 'No time to get formal.' She threw a look of pure venom towards the Doctor, who just smiled back benignly, blue eyes twinkling. 'And on a mere cardiologist's wage, you know . . .'

Professor Sullivan nodded, understandingly. 'Yes, it must be very difficult.'

Grace agreed. 'Well, we must circulate. See you around later.'

'Oh goodbye, Doctor. Doctors. Don't forget to try a glass of the Gioberti. It's a local wine, I understand.'

Grace moved away, muttering 'I hope it chokes you' under her breath and dragging the Doctor with her. 'So, this Master person. He's taken over Bruce's body, has he?' ·

'Unfortunately. However, it's starting to decompose and he'll need to take over mine before too long.'

'So, do you steal other people's bodies when you . . . you know . . . do what you did in the morgue?'

The Doctor shook his head.

'No, we don't die as such. It's when our bodies are too old to carry on, or injured beyond repair. The body literally reconfigures itself, using the existing cells but rearranging them, redistributing them. A Time Lord becomes what might appear to be a new man or woman but is in fact just a rearrangement of the old one. The brain stays the same, if a little muddled for a while.'

He laughed. 'I'll let you in on a secret some-time – if you promise not to tell anyone.'

All Grace could think about was the park, and the Doctor's sudden exhilaration as he regained his memory.

And their kiss.

'Later,' she said, pushing past another couple of party guests. 'Tell me about this Master. Why did he have to kill Bruce?'

'He's on his last life, literally. Time and time again he has found ways of prolonging his final incarnation. Each time, it's just been staving off the inevitable.' The Doctor looked down at his feet. 'And now he's realised that the only way to continue is to place his life essence into the one thing denied to him – another Time Lord's body. He's fighting to survive, Grace, and in that fight there are no rules.'

'You've known him a long time then?'

'Once – a very long time ago – we were friends. Almost brothers. We shared so many traits, so many ideals and so many frustrations. We both sought answers away from Gallifrey, but ended up diametrically opposed to each other.' The Doctor sighed and stuffed his hands into his pockets. 'It's rather sad really.'

Grace decided a morbid Doctor was the last thing she need right now. 'I've seen the way up to the clock, Doctor,' she said quietly. 'We only have about half an hour.'

'I know, Grace, but we'll need a security pass. The hatchway up there will be electronically locked, and I don't have my sonic screwdriver to open it.'

They were now standing by the roped-off area, the stairway to their left conveniently concealed to the majority of the guests, thanks to a curve in the wall.

'Here's our opportunity, Doctor,' said Grace suddenly, and waved towards a rather elderly man. 'It's Professor Wagg.'

Professor Wagg was wearing an evening suit that was probably last worn at a time when he was somewhat slimmer. His only hair was sticking out in little tufts above his ears and a pair of pince-nez were in danger of toppling off his nose. In his hands was a glass of white wine, some of which was slowly soaking into his shirt, and a few crumbs of smoked salmon bake appeared to have attached themselves to his beard. He, however, looked as if he did not care a jot – as if his philosophy was for people to take him as they found him. Grace, nevertheless, knew it was quite a manufactured image, and adored him even more for it.

Grace leaned back delightedly towards the Doctor but kept her attention on Wagg as his face dawned with recognition. 'He designed and built the clock. This whole thing is his baby.'

She moved forward, hugging Wagg. 'Lovely to see you, Joseph.'

'My dear Grace, what a pleasant surprise. I thought you Board people only turned up at Board meetings and the like.'

'Wouldn't miss a good party, now, would I?' Grace laughed with him. 'I've brought someone to meet you.'

'Young Brian is it? Been waiting for this. Give him the old once over, you know.'

Grace coughed. 'No, actually, Brian has . . . er, well, that is to say . . .'

'Didn't know the gift horse when he saw it, eh? Too bad. His loss.'

Wagg turned to the Doctor, holding his hand out. 'Joe Wagg. And you are?'

'A pleasure to meet you, Professor.'

'Oh,' Wagg raised his eyebrows and smiled at Grace. 'English. Good choice, Grace m'dear. Good blood in their veins.'

'He's a friend, Joseph,' sighed Grace, 'not a race-horse. This is Dr Beech, from London. He's got a secret to share with us.'

The Doctor grinned at Wagg and pointed straight up. 'Is there any chance of me getting a closer look at your delightful timepiece? I've always been a bit of a horologist.'

'No, I'm sorry, Doctor,' said Wagg. 'I'm afraid I'm the only person allowed up there.'

The Doctor put on his most seductive smile. 'Maybe you could bend the rules? Just a little?'

Wagg looked at the Doctor, then Grace, then back again to the Doctor. 'Well, possibly. Grace said you have a secret to share with us.'

The Doctor took Professor Wagg by the shoulder, as if to emphasise the conspiratorial nature of their conversation. He leaned forward and whispered into Wagg's ear. 'I am half-human. On my mother's side.'

There was a pause and then Wagg threw back his head and let out an enormous laugh. So loud that a lot of the guests stopped talking and turned to look in irritation. Grace noticed that once they

155

realised exactly who had laughed so outrageously, the little parasites smiled back as if they, too, were in on the joke.

'Grace,' Wagg said, 'I like this one.' He shook the Doctor's hand once again. 'Good to meet you, Doctor. I hope we'll meet again.'

'As do I, Professor, as do I. It's been a pleasure and an honour.'

'Oh, no, Doctor. The honour has been all mine.' Wagg patted his shoulder.

'Exactly.' The Doctor just smiled, and Wagg looked at Grace and then shrugged and wandered back into the crowd, still chuckling.

'So witty, Doctor, you're so witty,' and Wagg was swallowed up amongst his faithful and the hangers-on.

Grace looked straight at the Doctor and grinned.

The Doctor's face broke into a wide smile and he raised an eyebrow in triumph as he held his hand out. Nestling in the palm was a small plastic card, with an encrypted micro-strip along it.

'Joseph's security pass?' Grace was astounded. Pleased, but astounded.

'Sleight of hand.'

The Doctor flicked his head towards the stairway. 'Shall we go?'

Grace nodded and they climbed over the rope, checking no one had noticed them. Luckily all the other guests were too busy fawning over Professor Wagg or the television camera crews to notice much of anything.

The Doctor turned the corner and climbed the stairs, only to be confronted by a young security guard at the top. They were now standing in one of the glass corridors that linked the buildings which made up the Institute. Outside, the dark night was punctuated by the orange glow of downtown San Francisco, and the tiny moving lights.

'Beautiful view, isn't it?' the Doctor said.

The guard looked slightly bewildered. 'Yes, sir. May I ask what you're doing up here?'

Grace popped up from the stairs, waving Wagg's security pass. 'Professor Wagg and I were just checking up on the clock.'

She moved towards the closed hatchway, easing past the guard. 'If you don't mind . . .'

'Oh, yeah. Sorry.' The guard moved away and around the corner, scratching his head. He was sure something wasn't quite right, but he couldn't quite put his finger on it.

Grace slid the card through a slot and the hatchway slid back, revealing a tiny access area at the back of the atomic clock.

The Doctor was down immediately, using a tiny coin to unscrew the panel that would lead to the beryllium. 'As I said, where's my sonic screwdriver when I need it?'

He stopped and looked back at Grace and then pulled the straw hat out from under his coat. 'This used to be mine.'

'So?'

'So, it ought to have been with all my other things. Not my clothes, I know where they are. But surely the stuff in my pockets ought to have been put somewhere safe at the hospital?'

'Ah, yes, those things.' Grace tried not to look too embarrassed. 'They were, sort of, lost. Yeah, lost.'

'Lost?' The Doctor raised an eyebrow. 'Somehow I think "lost" is a bit of an understatement.'

'Oh, all right,' snapped Grace. 'I'm sorry. They were stolen. From my office. From in front of me.'

'Who by?'

'A Chinese boy. He was with you when you were shot. He travelled with Bruce in the ambulance.'

'And Bruce is now the Master,' mused the Doctor. He looked Grace straight in the eye. 'I wonder if he's working with the Master.'

The Doctor turned back to the panel. 'Oh, well, it couldn't be helped.'

Grace stared at is back as he struggled to undo the screws. She touched his shoulder. 'Hey, I really am sorry he got them.'

'As I said, it's not your fault. More sentimental attachment rather than practical use.' As the

Doctor twisted the coin, his other hand shoved the hat back under his coat.

The panel fell back and the Doctor steadied it. Grace peered in over his shoulder, but it resembled the inside of a computer to her. Human physiology she could find her way around blindfolded (so long as there weren't two hearts) but anything remotely electrical and she was lost.

The Doctor slowly inserted his finger into a tiny slot and eased out a wafer-thin silver strip of metal.

'Is that it?' asked Grace. 'The beryllium chip?'

'I told you it was small.' The Doctor held it out to her.

Grace smiled as she took it. 'Now, what is it they say about size?'

'They say that on my planet, too.' The Doctor began screwing the panel back into place.

'Sorted. Let's go.'

Gareth Fitzpatrick was sure he'd seen those two before. especially the lady with the strawberry-blonde hair. He stared out of the glass tube. The man was right, San Francisco was very beautiful at night. But there was something wrong –

'Hi, Gareth.'

He turned to see Sophie standing in the corridor, with a bottle of wine and two empty glasses in her hands.

'Sophie? Hi.'

'I thought I might find you here. Your friend David said you'd both been given corridor duty now that everyone had arrived. Professor Wagg gave me this to tempt you back downstairs. You must be off duty by now.'

'I don't know . . .'

What was he saying? How often did beautiful women offer him drinks?

'Is the Professor a friend of yours?'

'He's my father.'

That was it! 'Your father? Surely he's not old enough to be —'

Sophie frowned. 'What's up?'

'Where is your father right now?'

Sophie deflated slightly. 'Why does everyone want to meet my father and never me?'

'No, no, I do want to meet you.' Gareth stared at her. What was he saying? 'I mean, obviously I have met you, but I don't think I have met your father. He's not got long black hair and stupid clothes?' Oh, God, what if that was Sophie's father? He'd just insulted him magnificently.

'No.'

Thank God.

'No, Dad's about sixty with a beard and he's almost bald. Why?'

'Then there's an Englishman pretending to be him back there.' Gareth was torn between duty

160

and Sophie. 'Don't go away,' his mouth said, while his brain screamed out angrily "What are you doing?"

Gareth hurried back around the corner, just as the strawberry-blonde and the Englishman (a Dr Beech wasn't it?) emerged from the hatchway.

As they stood up, Grace smiled. 'Hello again. We're just going back down. Professor Wagg is happy with everything.' She glanced at her companion.

'And you were just saying how good you thought the security was, weren't you?'

'Oh, yes,' said the Englishman. 'Very adequate.' He suddenly stared hare at Gareth, who took a step back. 'I *do* know you, don't I?'

The blonde tugged at his sleeve. 'We spoke to him when we got up here. And in reception. Where I introduced you as Dr Beech,' she hissed.

She smiled apologetically at Gareth. 'He's a bit crazy tonight. It's the strain of all this.'

'You're Gareth Fitzpatrick, aren't you?'

Gareth stopped looking at the woman. Stopped thinking about how this man certainly was not Professor Wagg. Stopped wondering why they were fiddling with the atomic clock.

'Yes.'

'Gareth, you must answer the second question on your mid-term exam, not the third. The third may look easier, but you'll mess it up.'

'What?'

The Englishman grabbed Gareth's hand and shook it violently. 'Good to meet you, Gareth. Now remember: the second question. Don't forget!'

'Okay,' said Gareth slowly. How did this man know who he was? Or about his exams? 'Now, can I see what's in your hand please?'

The Englishman beamed. 'Good. An inquisitive mind. Useful to you one day.' He held his hands out. In it was a paper bag.

Gareth looked inside.

'Jelly babies. Have one. An English delicacy.'

Tentatively, Gareth took a green one and popped it in his mouth. He glanced back to where Sophie was still hopefully waiting around the corner. When he looked back to the hatchway, the Englishman and the blonde had gone.

How had he known who Gareth was?

'Gareth, are you coming?'

Sophie placed a hand on his shoulder. 'Or are you still thinking about my father? Should I get worried by this?'

Get your priorities right, Gareth Fitzpatrick. He smiled at her, captivated by her wonderful eyes, red lips, beautiful skin.

'Fancy that dance?' he said.

★ ★ ★

Grace and the Doctor were walking quickly along the transparent tubes, looking for a way back into the dining area below before finding themselves in another, locked, building.

Grace kept looking behind them, in case the young security guard showed up. 'What was that all about?'

'Gareth Fitzpatrick will head up the seismology unit of the UCLA task force ten years from now. He will devise a way of accurately predicting earthquakes.' The Doctor beamed at her. 'He's going to be very important.'

Grace looked back at him for a second, and then spoke slowly. 'You mean it, don't you?'

'Of course I do. His inventions ultimately save the human race several times. But first, he has to graduate in poetry.'

'Why?'

'Because that's the way these things work.'

The Doctor opened a door and they found themselves opposite the cordoned off area, some way from the clock, on a balcony overlooking the dining room. The exit, and the way to their motorbike, was therefore directly below them.

Grace touched the Doctor's sleeve. 'You are for real aren't you? I mean, I've been telling myself that this is all a dream. Something not quite real. Maybe I bumped my head, or I'm still at the Opera House with Brian.'

The Doctor moved back towards her, but she put her hand up to stop him. 'But it is absolutely real, isn't it? I'm stood here, talking to an alien who travels through time and space, trying to help him stop his old enemy from destroying Earth.' She shook her head. 'Have you any idea how difficult it is to rationalise that? To put together my training, my belief in science with something that's straight out of a bad fifties B-movie?'

The Doctor just carried on grinning. 'Believe it, Grace. Truth is always stranger than fiction.'

Grace nodded. 'I guess so.'

They looked down into the crowd.

'Half an hour until the millennium,' the Doctor said to break the silence. 'Give or take a few seconds as that clock tries to work without its major component.'

'Doctor,' Grace hissed. 'Down there!' She pointed towards the centre of the throng. 'There's Chang Lee, the boy who stole your things.'

As if sensing her, Chang Lee looked straight up and saw them, tugging on the sleeve of the man beside him.

Dark glasses. Dark suit. Paramedic's jacket.

'The Master's with him,' the Doctor said. 'We were right. We'd best get out of here.'

'How?'

The Doctor darted back out into the corridor. 'Straight up.'

Grace hurried towards him, and found him looking up a fire escape, leading to the roof. 'I hope you know what you're doing. They'll be here in a second.'

'No they won't.' The Doctor smashed his elbow into a fire alarm, breaking the glass and setting off what sounded like every alarm in the western world.

Grace stared at him. 'Why did you do that?'

'The party needed livening up, Grace. Come on!'

He hurried up the fixed ladder leading upwards, Grace following a couple of rungs below, using her foot to shut the door behind them. Every second that they could gain might be important.

Chang Lee looked from side to side, trying to track down the Master. He caught a glimpse of his partner nearing the far door, but the panicking crowds pulled them further apart.

For a moment he wondered if the Master would desert him, but remembered that he, and not the Master, had the ambulance keys.

By the far end of the room, below the clock thing, a bald man with a white beard was shouting and telling people not to panic. However, a moment later he vanished from sight, either knocked over by someone who was not listening, or giving up and running himself.

Chang Lee was right by the door now, and a rough security guard hauled him forward, almost throwing him into the cold air.

As he scrambled towards the ambulance, a black gloved hand grabbed his arm. 'Where were you, boy?' growled the Master. 'We must leave. The Doctor will be heading for his TARDIS.'

Grace stared down over the edge of the building. They were only four storeys up, but too far to jump.

'Grace,' called the Doctor from behind her. 'Grab this.'

She caught the brass end of a fire hose he was unspooling from inside the fire escape. 'You are joking!'

The Doctor pushed her over the edge and before she even had time to scream, Grace was plummeting downwards, gripping the unravelling hose, shooting faster and faster, the ground getting closer and closer.

At the last moment she screwed her eyes up tightly and prepared for impact.

Instead, the hose stopped suddenly. Slowly Grace opened her eyes – her feet were two inches off the top of a police car.

'Grace, let go!' the Doctor called from above.

She dropped and staggered forward, her heart beating faster than ever before.

She watched the Doctor shinning down the hose like an experienced abseiler and eventually he joined her.

Grace was not sure if she was going to hug him for his inventiveness or thump him for scaring her to death. She decided to do neither and they jumped off the car and began walking towards their abandoned motorcycle.

'Just how did you know exactly how long that hose was?' was all she managed to say, as he kick started the motorbike.

'I just made an educated guess,' he yelled as the cycle shot forward, weaving between frightened guests and guards fleeing the non-existent fire.

Grace caught a glimpse of Bruce's ambulance trying to drive between the same people but Chang Lee was obviously not prepared to simply run everyone over and the delay gave their cycle a good start.

Before long they were back on the bridge, heading for Chinatown, where the Doctor's TARDIS was meant to be.

'So,' she yelled. 'D'you know what's going to happen to me in ten years time?'

'You don't want to know,' was the reply.

'Yes I do! You can't not tell me!'

The Doctor just carried on driving. 'I'm sorry, Grace.'

'Oh, God,' Grace shouted, 'you don't mean

Brian's going to move back in? I mean, there are some things too horrible to contemplate!'

'I can't say, really.'

Grace was suddenly angry. He'd told that Gareth boy about his exams. He'd somehow known about her mother's death; her reasons for becoming a doctor. 'Please?'

The cycle was approaching a red light. Grace just knew they weren't going to stop.

They went straight through, once more almost causing a massive pile-up.

The Doctor turned left towards a sign that said CHINATOWN.

'The universe hangs by such a fragile thread of coincidence, Grace,' he said suddenly.

Grace smiled. He'd been actually considering her request.

'There's no point in trying to tamper with it unless, like me, you're a Time Lord.'

'Okay,' Grace agreed, 'just give me a few pointers, so that I can –'

There was the sudden wailing of a siren behind them, and Grace looked over her shoulder to see another motorcycle cop, red lights flashing, bearing down on them. 'We're being followed,' she cried.

'Not far,' said the Doctor as they went shooting down Jasmine Boulevard. He turned sharply into Rose Alley but all Grace could see was a tall, blue box. Which, in her considered opinion, looked very out of place.

The Doctor skidded to a halt and they jumped off, letting the cycle fall over.

'There she is!' The Doctor was almost hugging the blue box.

Grace read the sign printed on it. 'A Police Box? What's a Police Box?'

The Doctor was patting his empty pockets. He even whipped out his straw hat and looked inside that. The police siren was getting nearer.

Grace smiled. 'Now even I leave a spare key –'

'In a secret compartment above the door,' finished the Doctor. 'Grace, you're a genius.'

'Well, great minds think alike.'

'True.' The Doctor cupped his hands together. 'Come on, I'll give you a leg up.'

Sighing, Grace allowed herself to be propelled upwards, and ran her hands along the top of the TARDIS.

'There's a little cubby-hole above the capital "P".'

Sure enough, as Grace scrabbled about, her fingers found a tiny hole and inside was a piece of metal. She yanked it out and jumped back to the ground.

In her hand was a strangely shaped piece of metal, like a miniature trowel with a cross instead of a handle. 'This is a key?'

'Yes, thank you very much.' He started to open the TARDIS.

'Why a Police Box?'

The Doctor patted his box. 'Its chameleon circuit got stuck during a previous misadventure. I rather like it like this.'

'Very distinctive —' Grace began, but stopped as the police motorcycle turned into the alley, its siren screaming, blinding them with its headlight.

The Doctor shoved the doors to his TARDIS wide open and the police officer rode his cycle straight in.

Grace prepared herself for an almighty crash, but nothing happened. The Doctor began counting on his fingers and when he got to five, the cycle shot out again, its rider's eyes wide open in shock. The cop kept driving, as far away from Rose Alley as he could, his siren fading into the dull noise of the San Francisco traffic.

The Doctor pulled Grace into the TARDIS — and if she had possessed any lingering doubts, they vanished immediately.

'It's certainly large,' she said, noting the intricate candelabra and the wooden lectern. 'Been to a rummage sale recently, have we?'

The Doctor was at the central console, looking at what appeared to be an old Bakelite television screen suspended on a Z-spring. It showed the outside of the TARDIS and their abandoned bike.

He flicked a couple of gold rectangles into some slots and right on top of the console a holographic projection of something else appeared.

'The Eye of Harmony,' he said.

Grace realised she was rubbing at her arm and slipped her jacket off. Where the Master had spat venom at her, the skin had completely discoloured, going very green. A green rash was spreading further up her arm.

She opened her mouth to tell the Doctor but he was staring towards the massive library, his hand cupped to his ear, as if listening.

Faintly, Grace could hear a bell tolling.

'Hear that?' he asked her.

'Yes,' she replied, straining hard.

'It's a warning. The TARDIS is dying.'

He punched a button on the console. The exterior view of the TARDIS vanished, and was replaced by a blue screen, with the words *TIMING MALFUNCTION* flashing up on it.

'It's no good,' he said. 'We don't have enough auxiliary power to even move next door.'

The Doctor began rushing around the console, his hands moving in a blur as he moved, twisted, shoved and occasionally thumped everything he could. There was no doubt that he knew every piece, every square millimetre of the console, but his movements suggested he was getting more and more frustrated.

Eventually, he flipped a panel open and looked inside it.

'Sorry, old girl,' he muttered. Grace assumed he did not mean her, but was chatting to the TARDIS much as Brian used to do with his old car.

The Doctor clicked his fingers suddenly.

'Grace, the beryllium chip, please.'

Grace delved into her pocket and produced the tiny silver rectangle and passed it over. She tried to look inside the console without getting in his way, but quickly gave up, realising it was pointless. She had no hope of understanding any of it.

He suddenly pulled out a wooden box with a couple of frayed red wires attached to it. The beryllium chip was now lying on top, attached by a twisted paper clip.

'That looks a bit low-tech,' she said.

The Doctor did not look up as he replied, but continued attaching wires to the chip, and plucking other, run-down looking things out of the console. 'It's a Type 40 TARDIS. It can take me to any planet in the universe and to any date in that planet's existence.'

He shot her a look, beaming. 'That's temporal physics.'

Grace looked around her, things gradually making sense, in a bizarre, science-fiction way. 'You mean like inter-dimensional transference,' she offered. 'That would explain the spatial displacement we went through as we passed over the threshold.' All those lectures Professor Wagg had given on time travel hypotheses had obviously sunk in more than she'd believed.

The Doctor was smiling at her, like she was a prized student who'd passed all her exams with high marks. 'That sounds rather good,' he said. Then he turned and flicked a switch on the console. A little blue light beside the beryllium chip flashed. 'There,' he said.

The *TIMING MALFUNCTION* message vanished. And on the hologram, they could see the Eye of Harmony begin to close. The Doctor peered at something else on the console.

'Oh no,' he breathed, and thumped the console again. It obviously made no difference to whatever readings he was getting. He looked up to Grace, his eyes wide and frightened.

Just like his previous body had on the operating table. Eyes not used to fear . . .

'I've got a horrible feeling we're already too late.'

Grace looked at her watch.

'It's eleven forty-eight. We've still got eleven minutes.'

The Doctor punched a control and the holographic Eye vanished, to be replaced by a hologram of what Grace could only guess was the universe. It was beautiful – millions of dots of colour, swirls of gas clouds, yellow suns . . .

'There's no context,' muttered the Doctor. 'I'll have to check.'

'What are you doing?'

The Doctor was hunched over the console, his fingers tapping in commands, slipping golden squares and rods in and out of slots. 'I'm setting the coordinates for one minute after midnight. If I'm right, the Eye has already been open for too long and there is no future.' He shot a look at Grace. 'I only hope –'

He stopped as the hologram of the universe flared and vanished. 'Oh, no . . .'

Grace tried to make a joke of it all. 'Hey, you never said this thing was reliable.'

The Doctor ignored her. 'Whatever has started happening can't be stopped merely by shutting the Eye.'

'How come you didn't know that?'

'Because,' he said, 'I've never opened it before. It's like a miniature black hole, tapping into the real Eye of Harmony near Gallifrey. It exists both there and at the heart of every TARDIS simultaneously.' He shrugged. 'Frankly, it's too dangerous to open. It's like you driving your car down a freeway at seventy, climbing on to the hood and putting your hand into the heart of the engine. The chances are you'll lose your arm, the car will crash, explode and everyone in it will die. Not something you'd really consider doing.'

'Oh. Thanks.'

'Simply closing it hasn't been enough, Grace.'

He looked really worried and started tugging at a loose thread on his jacket sleeve, wrapping it around his finger.

'We have to go back,' he said suddenly. 'Back to before it was opened. Maybe before we even arrived.'

'Well,' Grace said, 'this is a time machine.'

'No power, remember? The Eye opening and closing has drained it all.'

'Oh, great.'

'I'm sorry —'

'You must have some more power. Or some way of getting the power back, at least. You simply must!'

Grace wanted to shake him, try and wake him up to the reality of all this. Whatever that was. Either way, standing around with a look of having given up all over his face was not going to help anyone.

'What about all your glorious predictions? All your knowledge of what is going to happen to that Gareth person? To me? To this city? That must come from somewhere!'

The Doctor looked blankly at her.

'Think!' she screamed at him.

When he moved towards her, it was so unexpected that Grace jumped. It crossed her mind that he was going to hit her. Instead, he grabbed both her hands.

'You're so right,' he said. 'Now, are you any good at setting alarm clocks?'

She remembered the countless time Brian had asked, last thing at night, if she had set the alarm for the morning. She, of course, answered yes only to wake up thirty minutes later than they ought to have. Brian, needless to say, resolved to take on alarm-clock duty after three months of hurried mornings.

'No,' she said truthfully.

'Oh, good grief,' the Doctor exclaimed.

'But I'll try,' Grace added hurriedly. She had got him doing something. There was no point in letting him give up again.

'Thank you,' he said wearily. 'Now, listen to me carefully.' He sat on the floor, pulling her down, and flipped open a compartment at the base of the console, yanking out a metal box with a handle across the top. He opened it to reveal futuristic things that could only be tools of some sort.

'We pre-set the coordinates,' he was saying. 'Then just as we divert the power from inside the Eye itself, it goes through into the time rotor, here.' He pointed inside the compartment.

'So,' Grace said slowly, 'to use your car analogy, we're jump-starting the TARDIS?'

'Sounds good to me.' The Doctor shoved his hand further into the compartment. 'Now, go over to the console where I placed the beryllium chip. Flip the top switch so that the blue light goes green.'

Grace nodded and stood up. She almost staggered. The sudden rise had made her light headed, and her vision blurred as she tried to find the beryllium chip. She reached forward to steady herself and noticed her hand had gone green.

That's not right, she thought.

Her head was hurting. There was a noise in her mind – a voice? – telling her something. She closed her eyes, but all she could see were two luminous green eyes, staring at her.

'Pass me the neutron rod, Grace.'

What was that? The Doctor? But he sounded so far away. The other voice, in her head was louder, more compelling. Commanding her attention.

'Kill the Doctor,' it said.

So simple a command.

'Kill the Doctor. Kill the Doctor.' The green eyes urged her on.

She opened her eyes. Everything around her had taken on a green hue, as if she were looking through tinted glass.

The Doctor's annoying voice moaned on again, demanding his neutron rod again.

Stupid man. Stupid TARDIS. Stupid neutron rod. The voice in her head was right.

'Kill the Doctor.'

Graced reached out and grabbed something off the top of the console and smashed the Doctor across the back of the head with it.

Soundlessly, he crumpled to the floor, dropping whatever it was he was wiring together.

'Very good, Miss Holloway,' said the voice in her head.

Except it was no longer in her head, it was in the TARDIS with her.

She turned to look. There, in the doorway was that Chinese boy. And beside him, green eyes glowing brightly, was the Master.

'Very good indeed.'

Six for gold

This body-swapping was really quite a fantastic thing, Chang Lee thought. It must be really cool to be able to leap around from face to face, always one step ahead of your enemies. No wonder the Master needed to catch the Doctor – some poor person had died so that he could take this new body.

Chang Lee was astonished at both the changes and yet the similarities between the two versions of the Doctor he had come into contact with.

This new one, currently strapped on to a gurney from Bruce's ambulance and being wheeled through the TARDIS corridors, was a bit younger and much taller. But the eyes were very alike and the mouth was the same. He wondered if the Doctor deliberately chose similar bodies, and thought back to the faces he had seen in the Eye of Harmony. There had often been the same nose or eyes, that had transferred from one face to another, as if the Doctor deliberately chose a certain style. Chang Lee reasoned it must be similar to people who moved house a lot; if you liked nineteenth-century architecture, you might add a room or two, or even go up a storey or two each time you moved, but your basic ideal remained the same.

Mind you, he was convinced that these two were definitely aliens. No one from Earth had the ability to build 'dimensionally transcendental' spaceships or body-swap. He was surprised at his own lack of fear about this. Maybe it was the novelty of it. After years of running with the gangs, anything new or unusual was cool, really. Maybe he'd stick with the Master afterwards. Sure, the guy could be bad tempered, but Chang Lee had dealt with worse. And anyway, once he'd got enough gold, he could buy the Master out.

Yeah, stick with the Master, get away from San Francisco and see a bit of the world. Or even the universe.

Chang Lee eased forward, leaning over the Doctor's unconscious body, past his attractive companion, and pushed open the wooden doors to the Cloisters.

That attractive companion now walked ahead, pulling the gurney. Chang Lee remembered the last time he had seen her; in her office, then chasing him through those hospital corridors. No contest. He had been running like that for years now, no one could ever catch him.

Now, here she was, silent and hypnotised by the Master, ready to do his bidding. Or Chang Lee's, perhaps?

As the cool, calm air of the Cloisters surrounded them, the Doctor stirred, groaning slightly.

Chang Lee stared down at him, wishing the Master would hurry back. All he had told Chang Lee to do was take the Doctor to the Eye of Harmony, where he would meet them later. Presumably the Master had not anticipated the Doctor's quick recovery.

They wheeled him down through the pillared walkways and into the cathedral, where the Eye lay, closed. Chang Lee stopped pushing the gurney and so Dr Holloway automatically stopped pulling. She just stood, facing forward, seemingly unaware of everything that surrounded her.

The Doctor's eyes popped open and he seemed to be taking in his surroundings.

He tried to lean back and clearly recognised Dr Holloway's back.

'Grace?'

Slowly, the woman turned and faced Chang Lee, looking straight over the Doctor, ignoring him.

The Doctor closed his eyes. 'Oh, no Grace, not you .. .'

Chang Lee smiled. Their captive was, at last, totally helpless.

The Doctor was wriggling slightly, as if trying to break the straps on the gurney. 'You know, Grace, this really is no time to be playing doctors and nurses.'

Chang Lee tapped his foot. 'It's no good talking to her. She's possessed.'

The Doctor peered up, trying to raise his head.

'Oh, it's you,' he said rudely and slumped back. 'You ran off with my things.'

He hauled himself up again, and Chang Lee thought he might have moved a fraction higher. He would have to check those straps.

The Doctor spoke again. 'So. Where are they?'

Instinctively Chang Lee's right hand tapped the pocket of his baseball jacket, feeling the bag secure inside.

The Doctor clearly noted this. 'Oh. At least they're safe then.'

'They're not your things any more.' Chang Lee tried to sound angry. 'Pretty soon everything around here's going to belong to the Master again.'

The Doctor just stared back. He had bright blue eyes that Chang Lee felt looked right through him. He shivered slightly. There was something about that look that suddenly made Chang Lee think harder about the Doctor. He did not seem particularly evil. He was not screaming or threatening Chang Lee. He certainly did not carry a gun or anything.

Of course he's evil, he told himself. This is just part of his tricks, to put you off guard.

'"Again"? What's the Master been telling you?'

Chang Lee leaned forward. 'You know, when he gets his lives back from you, when he has your body, I'm going to be rich.'

The Doctor nodded, understandingly. 'I see. And you believe him, do you?'

'Hey, everything about you two is weird enough already. Why shouldn't I? Can you make a better offer?'

The Doctor shook his head. 'Of course not. But I doubt he bothered to mention to you that there won't actually be anywhere left for you to spend all this money by the time he's finished?'

'And that's why we have no time to waste!'

Chang Lee turned to see the Master behind him.

'Time enough to change, I see,' murmured the Doctor.

Chang Lee turned to stare at his associate. He had removed his paramedic's jerkin and now wore a long black velvet cloak over his snake-skin suit. The cloak had a high collar at the back, and the whole thing was piped with a burnt orange. The collar itself was flecked with the same orange and as the Master stood on the wooden balcony over-looking the Eye of Harmony, Chang Lee felt a chill go through him. The Master suddenly looked as if he lived up to his name.

His face was very sunken, however, as presumably Bruce's body was almost spent. The skin had taken on an almost translucent look, with blotches of discoloured skin showing through the cheeks and around the eyes. The lips were split and one sore by his right ear was actually cracked and weeping slightly.

Chang Lee guessed that the Master did not really have much time left. He simply had to get his own body back before he finally died.

'I always like to dress for the occasion, Doctor, you know that.'

The Doctor snorted derisively. 'You always had a flair for the melodramatic. It's got worse as you've gone through lives.' He tried to sit up further. 'Thank you for the invite to your execution, by the way.'

'I knew you would come. You would not be able to resist seeing my defeat.' The Master turned to Chang Lee. 'See, my young friend, he even gloated at my misfortunes.'

The Doctor laughed wryly. 'Actually, I came to do the honourable thing. To take you home. My mistake.'

'Instead, you stole my life, bringing me to this planet where you could do the most harm.'

The Master clicked his fingers and Chang Lee and Dr Holloway moved towards the steps and walked up to join the Master on the balcony.

All three of them looked down at the Doctor.

'I never liked this planet, Doctor.'

'Just as well,' the Doctor retorted. 'Considering it will cease to exist any moment now.' The Doctor looked over to Chang Lee. 'What's the time, please?'

Chang Lee thought of the gold fob-watch in the bag. He reached into his jacket pocket and pulled the watch out.

The Master flicked his arm out, knocking the watch over the edge of the balcony and on to the wooden floor beside the Doctor.

'Time enough,' he said, 'to retrieve my rightful body and then get out of here.' He turned to Chang Lee, placing an arm around the boy. 'And take Chang Lee with me, of course.'

Chang Lee realised how little weight there was resting on his shoulders. The Master had to be standing, speaking and moving through vast amounts of pain and with huge reserves of resilience.

The Master smiled at Chang Lee, and the boy saw the sores around and in his mouth far more clearly. Most of the teeth had decayed and his breath was vile. 'You are the son I have always yearned for.'

'Oh, please,' groaned the Doctor from below. 'I think I'm going to be sick.'

Chang Lee suddenly felt very odd and disori-

185

entated. He took a slight step back from the Master. There was something very wrong, very frightening about what they were doing here.

In his mind's eye, he could still see the Master's reptilian green eyes. But they were losing their brilliance, as if they were fading away as Bruce's body died.

He felt as though something, some great weight, was lifting from his mind. But what did it mean? Surely he had wanted to stay with the Master, get rich and become that billionaire? In the pocket of his pants, he could feel the small bag of gold dust. Was that really what he wanted? Or had the Master somehow convinced him that was all there was in life?

Chang Lee needed to get away, he decided. He needed time to sort this out. Moments ago it had all seemed so right, so normal. Now, it was frightening him.

He stepped backwards down the steps and stood next to the Doctor's gurney, looking up at the Master.

The Doctor's fingers tapped his hand, and Chang Lee stared down at him.

'Chang Lee, this is *my* TARDIS. This is *my* Eye of Harmony. And I am in my *own* body.'

'Don't listen to him,' called the Master. '*I* am your friend.'

'The Master has run out of lives and now he

plans to steal mine. *That* is the truth!' The Doctor struggled. 'We have to stop him.'

The Master bellowed out another order. 'Move him into position, Chang Lee.'

Staggering slightly, he turned to Dr Holloway. 'Go and help the boy, Miss Holloway.'

As Dr Holloway descended the steps, Chang Lee looked from the Doctor to the Master.

The Doctor tapped his hand again. 'Look at Grace,' he hissed urgently. 'She is possessed by evil, not goodness.'

Dr Holloway now produced a weird object from behind her back and attached it to the Doctor's head. It was like a metal crown, with spikes sticking out from it. To this Dr Holloway calmly attached two curved arms. On the end of each one of these were two curved bits of metal. These were placed neatly around his eyes, like some nightmarish pair of spectacles. She turned a key on the rods and Chang Lee realised the Doctor's eyes were being forced open, and he swallowed, thankful that he had never caused the Master this kind of displeasure.

The Master leered down at the Doctor.

'This won't hurt, Doctor.' He smiled, showing his decayed teeth and bleeding gums. 'Well, not much anyway.'

★ ★ ★

Shelly Curtis, in her Georgian gown and wig, looked out of the room where the party was in full swing, searching for Jim Salinger.

Angela Wheeler came up behind her. 'Marvellous job they've done in here,' she said, brushing a few crumbs of cake off her pink bunny costume.

Shelly let the door close. 'Yeah, I knew this old ward would come in handy for something.'

She sighed quietly and Curtis noticed that Pete from the mortuary was wandering drunkenly towards them. He was dressed, he had claimed, like Richard Nixon but, in fact, looked just like an inebriated Pete in a suit. Still, thought Curtis, that was pretty fancily dressed for him.

'I originally wanted to be an Edwardian suitor,' he burbled, 'but someone stole my cravat.' He breathed what smelled like half a bottle of Bourbon over the two of them.

'Very sad, Pete,' smiled Wheeler. 'But you weren't the only one, were you?'

Ted, also from the mortuary, hurried over, his Wild Bill Hickok costume notably missing its frock coat. 'Hey, Pete, your Barbara's getting off with Batman over there.'

With a snarl, Pete hobbled back the way he came.

Ted smiled at the two nurses. 'She's not really,' he said soberly, 'but I know what he's like when he's had too much. And you two looked like you needed rescuing.'

Curtis smiled. 'Thanks. Seen Jim Salinger yet?'

'No. He's going to miss the big twelve if he doesn't get a move on.'

Curtis glanced at the clock. It read 11.55.

Ted was still talking to Wheeler, explaining how he and Pete had moved all the beds and scaffolding out earlier that afternoon and set the party up, when Jim Salinger bustled in.

He was still trying to get his Lone Ranger mask in place, and looked very harassed. 'I've tried calling Grace,' he said, 'but there's no answer. I thought she had a machine?'

Curtis shrugged. 'If Brian's walked out, he probably took it. He struck me as the kind who would.'

'Right.' Salinger glanced around, nodding appreciatively. He tapped Ted's shoulder. 'Good job you've done in here, Ted. Thanks.'

'My pleasure.' Ted and Wheeler rejoined the main throng, preparing to get champagne ready for the stroke of midnight.

Curtis kissed Salinger's cheek. 'Happy New Year, Jim.'

'It will be if you do that more often,' he replied.

'Uh-uh,' she said. 'You're not my type.'

'I'm fully house-trained,' he protested.

'Yeah, and I bet you say that to all the girls,' Curtis grinned. 'I'm sure you are, but my husband might object, and you wouldn't want to pick an argument with a construction worker, would you?'

'Guess not,' Jim laughed.

'Come on.' Curtis dragged him towards Angela Wheeler. 'Let's party!'

Within the massive society party at the Institute of Technological Advancement and Research, Professor Joseph Wagg stood on the podium.

After the excitement of the false fire alarm, he was relieved to still be there. He was staring out at the expectant sea of faces, all waiting to hang on his every word, to cheer and applaud every time he so much as breathed loudly or coughed. He was a little more interested in making sure the newscasters got it all, and he shifted his position so he was more directly in line with the cameras.

'Ladies and Gentlemen. Friends and associates. Tonight, you are here to witness the culmination of my life's work.'

He caught a glimpse of his daughter and some pleasant looking young man just to the side of the podium, out of sight on the stairwell leading to the clock. The young man was whispering to Sophie and he saw her eyes grow larger in surprise.

Professor Wagg crossed his fingers and hoped nothing was going to spoil his big moment.

★ ★ ★

Next door to Grace's apartment, Mrs Trattorio hugged her cat, listening to it purr.

She took a sip of her brandy and settled back to see the millennium in with KKBE, and their live broadcast from the Institute. It was a proud day for San Francisco.

She turned slightly and silently toasted a photograph on the sideboard. It showed a handsome young man in an Italian army uniform, smiling broadly.

'Happy New Century,' she whispered.

Her cat snuggled up in her lap, purring even louder.

Officers Selby and Buffini watched as the bagged body was taken out to the ambulance waiting in the street below.

A group of neighbours were staring in shock, preparing to see in their new year with a drama.

Poor Mrs Gerhardt, they were all muttering. What a terrible tragedy. And where was the lovely Bruce? Surely it couldn't be true, what the police were suggesting? That that nice Mr Gerhardt, the caring paramedic, had murdered his own wife.

They were – had been – such a lovely couple, with so much to look forward to in the twenty-first century.

★ ★ ★

The possessed Dr Holloway was helping Chang Lee to haul the struggling Doctor across the wooden floor of the cathedral, and over towards the Eye.

The Time Lord had put up enough of a struggle to kick the gurney over, but a well placed thump to the back of the neck by Chang Lee had momentarily stunned him enough for Dr Holloway to whip the straps off the gurney and tie him up with them.

'Up here, my friends,' goaded the Master, indicating that they should bring him to the balcony overlooking the Eye of Harmony.

As the Doctor began to struggle again, Dr Holloway pushed him forward and on to his knees.

Chang Lee then helped her lift him up bodily and push him against the ornate lattice-work, directly above the stairs, his face level with a carving of that Rassilon guy.

'Binding me up like this won't help you,' the Doctor muttered weakly.

However, Dr Holloway took his left arm and threaded the straps through the ornate lattice-work and around his wrist. Chang Lee did the same to his right wrist and moments later both his legs were similarly bound.

The Master was on the floor next to the Eye of Harmony now, looking up at his prisoner, held on to the upper wall by just the four straps. Chang

Lee could see the delight on the Master's face, and the pain on the Doctor's.

The gold in his pocket seemed heavier than ever before.

'You know, I always claimed you were a Universal Man, Doctor. Leonardo da Vinci would have been proud.'

'Oh, very amusing,' the spread–eagled Doctor said through gritted teeth. 'Your sense of humour is as warped as poor Bruce's spent body. Are you dead yet?'

The Master just chuckled.

The Doctor tried to hold his head up, but both gravity and Dr Holloway's surgical vice made it fall forward. 'In seven hundred years no one has ever opened the Eye of my TARDIS. How, then, did you do it?'

'Simple,' cackled the Master. 'Chang Lee is human. And you are only half.'

The Master indicated that Chang Lee and Dr Holloway should come back down. As they joined him, all three crossed to the mirror sceptres, moving all but the one that Chang Lee had removed earlier into a new arrangement.

'Perfect,' the Master coughed. 'Just perfect.'

He crossed to the foot of the steps and reached up with an unsteady hand, as if to bless the Doctor's far away feet. 'A new body, at last, Doctor. My gratitude.'

He began climbing the stairs, looking back over his shoulder.

'Open the Eye of Harmony, Chang Lee, while I prepare myself for a new lease of life.'

Chang Lee began to approach the energy beam still bleeding from the sceptre mirror he had taken away earlier, and as he did so, his eyes locked with the Doctor's.

And all he could think about was how uncomfortable he was with all that gold dust in his pocket.

Mrs Trattorio was watching her television with her cat, who now shared his place on her lap with the photograph of the young Italian soldier.

Mrs Trattorio's finger was caressing one corner of the photograph, where in faded ink was inscribed a message.

To my darling Gigi,

The war may have parted us for now, but I will be with you again soon.

I love you.

Bruno.

November, 1944.

On the television screen, Professor Wagg was tapping his glass.

'Ladies and Gentlemen,' he was saying, 'both here at the Institute of Technological Advancement and Research and the millions watching us at home, it is three minutes to midnight. In exactly one hundred and eighty seconds, the world will enter a new millennium. And with it, a new standard of accuracy will come to show how we measure time.'

He stopped as a pretty young lady tapped him on the shoulder.

He threw a quick look at the television cameras, and smiled. 'Excuse me, my daughter has something to tell me.'

Mrs Trattorio tutted, and looked at her watch.

From out of the television she suddenly heard a gasp from Professor Wagg.

'What d'you mean, "it won't start"?'

Chang Lee was staring straight ahead, knowing that any second now the Eye would open again and its power would be directed as the Master had arranged, straight into the Doctor's forced-open eyes, effectively stealing his life from him, back into the Master's own form.

His friend would have his proper body back.

Or would he? Why was this suddenly so confusing?

'This is your last chance, Chang Lee,' called the weakened Doctor.

'No, Doctor,' he replied, trying to sound cool. Relaxed. 'This is my *only* chance.'

He placed his face towards the energy. All he

had to do was actually enter it and he would soon be hearing the Eye of Harmony open once more. He would also hear all the energy flooding upwards, spreading outwards and the Master would live again.

The Master jeered at the Doctor.

'He's right, Doctor. There is nothing for him here. He has no family, no real friends and no future. Only death awaits him on the streets outside. But with me as his guide and mentor, he'll get to see the entire universe.'

The Doctor tried to move, to look down at the Master. 'This is his last chance to stay alive, and you know it.'

The Master stepped back quickly, almost shouting. 'What do you know of last chances, Doctor?'

'More than you.'

'Oh, you're so insufferably good, aren't you Doctor?' The Master was screaming now. 'Always ready to sacrifice yourself for the good of everyone else. You sanctimonious hypocrite – why aren't you willing to sacrifice yourself for me?'

The Doctor was looking at Chang Lee again, but all he could do was watch the Master, mesmerised by his sudden outburst.

And Chang Lee felt his mind clearing.

The Doctor spoke softly, but Chang Lee still heard him.

'Because you're not worth it.'

The Master slammed his fist against the lower wall. 'I have wasted all my lives because of you, Doctor. Now I will be rid of you.'

The Doctor jerked forward, smiling suddenly.

'*All* your lives, Master? Didn't you tell Chang Lee over there that I had stolen all your lives?'

Chang Lee stared at them both. The green eyes in his head were gone, and he suddenly realised everything. He had been used. Twisted, bribed and mesmerised into doing what the Master wanted.

But there was still all that gold.

'Don't listen to him.' The Master suddenly seemed back in control of his temper.

The Doctor shouted loudly. 'No, don't listen to him, Chang Lee. He has used up all his lives and now he wants to steal mine. Like I told you, this is my TARDIS and this is my body.'

The Master pointed at Chang Lee, his face twisted in fury. 'Open the Eye of Harmony, Chang Lee! I am your Master. Obey me!'

Chang Lee looked at the Doctor. He then looked at Dr Holloway, standing below the Doctor, possessed. The Doctor's friend, forced against her will to hurt him and cage him, peeling his eyes back. That had to be agony for the Doctor.

Was he like that? Was that what he had become? Had life in the gangs really made him so easy to manipulate, so greedy for the next buzz, the next thrill, that he would ally himself with anyone?

'Open the Eye!' the Master screamed.

'No,' Chang Lee screamed back. 'No, you lied to me!' He moved away from the Eye. 'You are evil!'

The Master threw back his head and then spat viciously, sending a massive green globule of venom straight across the Cloister room. It hit Chang Lee in the chest and he felt himself burn, falling backwards.

A second later, his eyes focused. He was not dead, but his chest hurt like crazy. He could see the steps in front of him, and guessed he was lying against one of the massive doors leading outside.

He realised he was paralysed, completely and utterly. He tried to speak, to blink, anything, but he could not move a muscle. All he could do was look straight forward, at the Doctor suspended off the upper wall, Dr Holloway on the floor below and the Master hurrying towards the balcony, waiting for the energy to reflect out of the Doctor and engulf him.

The Doctor was angry. 'If you've hurt him . . .'

'You'll what?' sneered the Master. 'What will you do, Doctor? Shout about it?'

The Doctor let out a deep breath, then spoke calmly. 'How are you going to open the Eye now?'

The Master leaned over the balcony, looking directly down at Dr Holloway.

'Grace!'

Slowly she turned and looked up at him.

'Don't move.'

The Master staggered down the steps again, using the last vestiges of energy in Bruce's re-animated corpse. He then hobbled towards Dr Holloway.

'Unless I'm much mistaken,' the Doctor smiled, 'that won't work in her present state of mind.'

'How right you are, Doctor,' the Master replied. 'Watch.'

He leaned forward and over Dr Holloway's face. He seemed at first to be kissing her, but Chang Lee realised he was actually sucking the poison back out of her. As he did so, her skin returned to its proper colour.

'No,' the Doctor shouted. 'No, Grace!'

Dr Holloway staggered slightly, and the Master stepped back from her, his green eyes glowing brightly, infused with energy again.

'Shut your eyes, Grace!' yelled the Doctor, but it was no good. Dr Holloway was staggering, as if awoken and trying to get her bearings. The Master just grabbed her by the hair and shoved her face into the Artron energy, spilling it outwards, where it began reflecting off the other mirrors.

The Eye of Harmony opened. Its own energy

poured out in a noisy rush and joined the light, beaming straight into the unblinking eyes of the Doctor.

The Master let her go and hurried back up the steps, to stand directly before the Doctor and receive the energy as it shot through him, transferring the Doctor's lives into him as it did so.

Dr Holloway, fell to the ground, crying.

'Blind,' she moaned. 'Oh, my God, I've gone blind!'

'Your sight will return, Grace,' the Doctor shouted above the noise of the energy flow.

Slowly she looked up, but it was too late. The energy was already entering the Doctor's eyes and then out and into the Master.

'Ah, yes,' the Master smiled. 'That's better.'

Grace Holloway gazed up at the scene before her. The Doctor strapped above a ornate wooden balcony, that Master person in front of him, and bright beams of energy shooting around them.

'What the hell's going on?'

She moved away from the pillar of energy beside her, and saw Chang Lee crumpled against one of the distant doors, his eyes wide open, his chest horribly burned and stained green.

'Grace,' came a croak from above.

'Doctor?' She could not understand how one minute she had been helping him in the console room and the next, everything had gone mad. 'What's happening?'

'The Master . . . he can't move. As long as the Eye links us. Remember Grace . . .'

'"Re-route the power." Yes, I remember.'

The Doctor was in agony. 'In the console room. Go!'

Grace started to move but turned back. 'But you'll die if I leave you!'

'And we'll all die if you don't. Please! Go!'

Beside her, the huge flat Eye was opening wider, casting more light on both the Doctor and the Master.

'Run, Grace. Run!'

She ran, somehow knowing which was the right way to go.

She did not look back, but could hear the Master's maniacal laughter as he screamed in ecstasy. 'I can hear your thoughts, Doctor. I can feel your memories!'

The party at Walker General was in full swing.

'Thirty seconds, Shelly,' said Jim Salinger. 'You don't need a construction worker when you've got me.'

Shelly Curtis smiled and grabbed at Pete as he drunkenly staggered past. She kissed him hard on the cheek and he smiled brightly.

'Wow!' Pete turned away and walked straight

into Lana from reception, dressed in a shroud from the mortuary, her face painted like a skull.

He fainted.

Shelly Curtis was looking at Salinger. 'Sorry, Jim. But Happy New Century anyway!'

Mrs Trattorio hugged her purring cat a little tighter.

'Happy New Century,' she said, kissing its head.

The cat looked up and licked her hand.

Everyone at the Institute was partying wildly. Professor Wagg stared mournfully up at his failed clock, and then back at his guests.

He saw his beautiful daughter, Sophie, dancing with that young man she'd been with earlier. Gareth something, she had said. She was leaning forward and kissing him.

Professor Wagg was going to frown, then shrugged. 'Girls will be girls,' he muttered. He looked again at his clock, and then at his wrist watch.

'Oh, what the hell,' he said. 'Twenty. Nineteen. Eighteen . . .'

The other party-goers took up the chant.

'Seventeen. Sixteen.'

Sophie and her young man parted, both grinning from ear to ear.

'Fifteen. Fourteen.'

Champagne corks popped, people yelled and pumped hooters.

'Thirteen. Twelve.'

All across San Francisco, cars in the streets slammed on their horns in a huge cacophony of celebration.

Officer Buffini finished marking out her chalk figure of where Miranda Gerhardt had been found.

She looked over to Officer Selby. 'How long?'

Selby grinned and pointed to his watch.

'Eleven. Ten.'

Shelly Curtis was hugging Ted, Angela Wheeler and Jim Salinger.

'Group hug!' she shouted and loads of other guests moved towards them, making a huge ball of people in the centre of the room, all shouting.

'Nine. Eight. Seven.'

'Happy New Century,' yelled Salinger. 'It's gonna be great!'

'Six. Five. Four. Three. Two. One. Midnight!'

The world died as time imploded, wiping out everything on Earth in a millisecond, reversing it as if it had never even existed.

Reality throughout the space/time continuum

shuddered and heaved as one small planet and the all the effect it had ever had, or ever would have, on the rest of the universe ceased to be.

Reality changed.

And the planet Earth was gone.

Trapped in the Cloisters of his own TARDIS, the Doctor felt an enormous rush of energy pour through the Eye of Harmony in one second.

It engulfed him and the Master, and for a nanosecond everything turned negative.

'This can't be how it ends,' he shrieked. 'Stop this! Please!'

Everything went white.

Seven for a secret never to be told

Grace was thrown from side to side as she tried to find her way through the maze of TARDIS corridors. Somehow, she guessed that either the Doctor's mind, or possibly the TARDIS itself, was guiding her in roughly the right direction.

All she could think about was the trapped Doctor, and what he had said in the park.

'If I look into the Eye of Harmony, my soul will be destroyed. The Master will be free to take my body then.'

And that was what she had seen beginning back in that weird cathedral place.

Every so often, she'd have a sudden blur of recognition and realised that there was only one explanation for her presence beside the Eye of Harmony. She must have been taken there by the Master, possibly enslaved by him.

Her freedom explained why her arm no longer carried the stain of the poison.

She felt awful. But there was little point in

focusing on that right now – the most important thing was to stop the Master. Once that was done, she would find some way to deal with this violation.

The TARDIS bucked violently, hurling her through an arched doorway, and she found herself in the console room.

Whatever the Master had started was now in the full throes of execution. She didn't have long.

'Please, God,' she muttered, half thrown, half throwing herself to the floor and rolling to the base of the console arches. She hauled herself up the tiny steps and round to the open hatch the Doctor had been working on earlier.

Across the room, books were tumbling from the Library, pages ripped out by the forces whipping through the room. The lectern was on the floor, the eagle snapped away and the candelabra was also down, the everlasting candles in danger of setting book pages alight.

Abandoned there was the beryllium chip, attached to whatever it was the Doctor had attached it to. 'Re-route the power,' she muttered. 'Just re-route the power.' She pulled some wires out.

'How?'

She began attaching various wires to the beryllium chip's new home, but the TARDIS lurched suddenly and gave her a slight shock.

After a few moments, she was getting nowhere, and could feel tears of frustration and anger welling up. 'No,' she shouted at no one in particular. 'No, I won't let this beat me.'

Chang Lee felt a tingle down his right arm, and he tried to move his fingers. The effort was excruciatingly painful, but he felt his little finger lift a fraction.

The paralysis was not going to be permanent. That meant he had to find the strength, not just to get up, but to help the Doctor defeat the Master.

To atone for what he had helped do.

He watched as the Master soaked up more of the energy burning through the Doctor. He was laughing, almost screaming with pleasure.

'Alive!' he cried. 'I am alive!'

The Doctor was barely moving.

Before him, on the balcony, the Master began to blur and change. Chang Lee watched in horrified fascination as he seemed to split down the middle, his clothes and Bruce's body flopping uselessly to the stone floor, discarded. In their place, the Master was just a silhouette of a man, arms stretched up, head thrown back. The silhouette flickered briefly, filling up with the images Chang Lee had seen in the cathedral the last time the Eye of Harmony had been opened – planets, stars, swirling gas clouds. As if the universe was contained within the humanoid outline of the Master.

Seconds later, the silhouette began to glow, leaving the Master standing as a solid white figure, a sort of bleached out reflection of the Doctor's outline. Chang Lee could see the coat tails trailing in the wind, the cravat undone and blowing loosely around his neck. Gradually a face began to form; featureless, like an incomplete clay model.

Chang Lee managed to raise his whole hand. If he could stand between the Doctor and the beams, try and cut them off . . .

Grace had run out of wires to check, to link up. She slammed her fist against the side of the vibrating wooden console angrily.

A red wire flopped down from inside – one she had not touched before.

'Please!' She attached it to the beryllium chip and a massive spark sent her flying back down the steps. The lights in the console room dipped dramatically but the vibrating stopped.

She could hear the Cloister Bell pealing out its mournful lament.

The top of the console suddenly flared white, and a wave of heat washed across her. She smelled burning and saw that the wire and the beryllium chip was distorting under the heat.

'No!' she shouted impotently, as if it would stop at her command.

Then the time rotor atop the console began to

rise and fall, accompanied by a bizarre wheezing and groaning sound.

Slowly, as the heat and light around the console faded, Grace lifted her head up, gazing over at the monitor suspended above her. The facia was cracked and pitted, and the glass screen was fragmented.

On the console in front of her, the figures on a digital clock began racing round.

'What now?' she wondered.

Chang Lee was desperately trying to move when the light from the Eye diminished suddenly.

'She did it,' the Doctor breathed. 'Grace! You did it!'

He stared down at the Master, his face racked with pain, but his forced-open eyes blazing in triumph. 'Your life-force is dying, Master!'

'No,' came an unearthly gurgling screech nearby. It could only be the Master, but he was mid-transformation, unfinished and indistinct. He stumbled down the steps, towards the Eye. 'More power! I need more light. I'm nearly there!'

Grace was frantically punching at the console, twisting dials and sliding rods and rectangles into the antique-looking slots, trying to stop the clock. 'Think alarm clock, Grace,' she shouted at herself. 'Think alarm clock!'

She inserted a few more rods and punched some more switches. 'Professor Wagg never taught anything like this!'

The screen above her suddenly flashed a new message:

ENTERING TEMPORAL ORBIT.

'What the heck is a temporal orbit?' She hit the console and the clock stopped moving. 'How am I supposed to understand any of this?'

As the clock had stopped, she turned and ran out of the console room to see if she had made any difference back at the Eye of Harmony.

She could have sworn that the journey back was shorter than before, but as she hurled herself towards the wooden doors of the cathedral, she realised that it hardly mattered. She ran in, noting Chang Lee still slumped to one side – dead or alive, she had no way of knowing. The Doctor was still moving however, and the light from the Eye of Harmony was still beaming into him, but with notably less force.

Of the Master there was no sign, but she could see a smouldering pile of something on the balcony, just at the top of the steps. Shocked by her vengeful thoughts, she hoped that he had got what he deserved and that was all that was left of him.

She dashed up the steps and then clambered up the wall, holding on with one hand as she started undoing the Doctor's caged head. Seconds later, he was able to close his eyes, as tears streamed down his face. She threw the hideous contraption over her shoulder, and then began concentrating on his bound wrists.

She was between the Doctor and the Eye now, and could feel the light beaming into her. But at least she was shielding him.

The Doctor opened his eyes, and grinned weakly. 'You did it, Grace. Well done.'

'Doctor!' She changed hands, now loosening his other wrist. 'Doctor, what is a temporal orbit?'

'Why?'

'Because we're in one.'

He gripped the lattice work as she bent down to release his feet. 'Grace!'

His warning was too late. Grace felt her ankle grabbed from behind. She twisted around and came face to face with . . . something.

It was a brilliant white figure of a man, but with no defined edges within its shape. She could see the outline of a collar, and the tail of a coat behind, but it looked liked a traced drawing.

Only the face had any substance — it was a lumpy, unmade face, with half-closed eyes and a snarling mouth.

However, when it spoke, she immediately recognised the Master's voice.

'What have you done, woman!'

He tugged her to the floor and before Grace could stagger away, he picked her up and hurled her down the steps.

Grace tensed herself for a bad fall, and heard a dull crack as something snapped. Probably a rib or two, hopefully nothing more serious. She lay for a second, mentally checking herself. She was still breathing hard but without difficulty. Her lungs had not been punctured. It might be painful, but she could still move around.

As she staggered to her feet, she saw the Master dashing down the steps and the Doctor, now free of his bonds, drop to the ground, facing the bizarre new version of his sworn enemy.

The Master reached out, picking up a sceptre that someone had moved out of its plinth. He swung it at the Doctor, who jumped up and over it. The sceptre thudded into the wall below the balcony, shattering the mirror, sending shards of glass everywhere.

Grace hurried over towards Chang Lee. She felt him touch her hand. 'Are you okay?' she asked, but the only response was a squeeze of her hand. 'Okay, I'm sorry, but I'm going to try and help the Doctor. See if I can distract the Master. I'll try and help you later.'

She stood up. 'If there is a later,' she muttered.

The Master, using the sceptre like a fighting staff, slashed at the Doctor again and again. The

Doctor was getting weary; Grace guessed that he had only a third of his normal energy after the battering from the Eye of Harmony's light.

Then he fell back and the Master brought the sceptre crashing down. The Doctor had feinted, however, and rolled aside as the sceptre smashed into the side of the Eye, splitting in two.

The Doctor rolled forward, grabbing the other half of the sceptre with both hands. *'En garde!'* he cried, thrusting forward like a fencing champion.

The Master parried successfully and the Doctor fell back, dodging round the other side of the Eye.

Both Time Lords were now hidden to each other, the solid light from the Eye shooting straight up.

Grace ran to the Doctor's side, but he pushed her back.

'It's too dangerous, Grace. He'll kill you.'

'Think!' Grace shouted back. 'There must be something I can do?'

The Doctor quickly pointed at the hole where the sceptre ought to have been.

'We need to cut off the energy supply and close the Eye.' He passed her his half of the pole. 'Block it up!'

She dashed towards it, shoving the damaged sceptre back in, ignoring the searing light and energy rushing past her.

Immediately, the light beams cut off, and the

mirrors ceased reflecting. But it was too late to stop the Eye itself — instead of closing, more energy shot up and both Time Lords staggered back.

'You can't win, Doctor,' screamed the Master. 'My body is new, fresh and strong. Yours is weak. Dying.'

'Oh, rot!' the Doctor called back. 'I'm fine and you know it. You, on the other hand . . . Well, try looking in a mirror if you don't believe me!'

The Master quickly dived forward, just missing the beam of light and careered into the Doctor, both of them rolling back.

The Doctor was staring up into the Master's face, a sneer on his lips. 'You want dominion over the living, yet all you ever do is kill.'

The Master laughed. 'Life is wasted on the living, Doctor.'

He jumped up and grabbed the Doctor's collar, hauling him back into the beam of light, face first.

Grace went to move forward, but stopped as the Doctor suddenly went limp. The Master obviously over-compensated, and pushed the Doctor's body in the wrong direction, dropping him and staggering forward.

The Doctor was free, and the Master had made his last mistake. His momentum carried him straight into the the Eye of Harmony, the light hurling him upright into the air.

The Doctor tried to reach out for him, but the Master was too far up, twisting and screaming in anger and pain, caught in the beam of pure energy from the very heart of the Eye of Harmony.

Grace watched as his body was buffeted by the light, and then it started to stretch. The Master was getting thinner and longer, his screams fading until, in a brilliant flash, he simply ceased to exist.

The Doctor moved to Grace, pulling her away and nearer to Chang Lee.

The light began billowing outwards, filling the area completely with golden brilliance and all Grace could hear was the Cloister Bell, ringing incessantly in her ears.

For a brief moment, she thought she could see her mother, smiling, waving to her.

Grace's hands were glowing with the light, and she suddenly felt the pain in her chest fade, and her energy begin to return.

The light faded from the cathedral walls and floor and she blinked a few times to clear her vision.

She realised the Doctor was hugging her tightly and she could feel his breath on her neck, smell his hair. She tapped his shoulder and, grinning, he pulled back.

'Hello,' he said.

'Hi,' she replied. 'Is that it?'

'That is a powerful force, the Eye of Harmony.

Normally, any non-Time Lords should have been totally vapourised. You two did something I've never done.'

'What's that?'

'You cheated death. How does that feel?'

Grace smiled. 'It's nothing to be afraid of.'

She reached out and hugged him again. Over his shoulder, she saw the Eye of Harmony close.

The Doctor turned just in time to see this too.

'Incredible!' He jumped up. 'What a sentimental old girl the TARDIS is!'

Grace began to relax. 'Think I figured out what we did.'

The Doctor sat cross-legged in front of her.

Chang Lee groaned and shook his head. His chest was healed and in his hands was the bag containing the Doctor's personal effects.

'These are yours,' he said, a little sheepishly.

'Thank you, young man. Good to have you back in the land of the living.' The Doctor patted his knee. 'Now listen. Grace is going to tell us how she saved the universe.'

Grace swallowed. 'Okay. That thing on the console isn't just a clock, is it?'

'No.'

'It's some kind of chronometer. And a temporal orbit is like being dragged back in time but not space.'

'You're getting there. A little basic, but it'll do.'

'Okay. So what you got me to do, what you needed that beryllium chip to power, was to move this TARDIS of yours back to a point before the Eye was first opened. Therefore giving you enough time to close it without doing any real damage.' Grace folded her arms. 'Well?'

The Doctor looked at Chang Lee. 'What do you think, Chang Lee?'

'Don't ask me, Doctor. I don't understand any of it.'

'Did we go back far enough though?' Grace asked.

The Doctor. 'Must have done. Or I'm talking to a couple of ghosts.'

Ten minutes later, they were standing in the console room. The Doctor was hunched over the console itself, pressing buttons and wiping it down. The screen was no longer cracked, and the hologram of the universe was once again rotating above the time rotor.

'Where's the Master?' asked Chang Lee.

The Doctor pointed at the hologram. 'Let's just say his plan never saw the light of day.'

He twisted a dial on the console and a strange grumble came up from the depths of the TARDIS. 'Oh, indigestion, poor old girl. Must have swallowed something that disagreed with her.' He smiled. 'Now, let's see where we are.'

He peered at the universe. 'Well, now, the future is roughly −' he pointed vaguely in the middle − 'thataway.' His finger moved across the representation. 'And that's home − on the other side of your galaxy.'

'Gallifrey?'

'Gallifrey. Home. That has a nice ring to it.' He looked at them both. 'It's two hundred and fifty million light years away. About ten minutes in this old thing.' He patted the TARDIS console.

'So, where are we now? Or rather, when?' Grace wandered over to a little seat near the fish pond.

'December 29th, actually.' He smiled at her. 'Want to get off here?'

'And go through all that again?' muttered Chang Lee. 'No, thank you. I wouldn't survive it.'

Grace thought for a moment. 'No. It means Brian would be at the apartment. And I can do without that, thank you.' She smiled. 'No, let's go and see the future.'

The party at Walker General was in full swing.

'Thirty seconds, Shelly,' said Jim Salinger. 'You don't need a construction worker when you've got me.'

Shelly Curtis smiled and grabbed at Pete as he drunkenly staggered past. She kissed him hard on the cheek and he smiled brightly.

'Wow!' Pete turned away and walked straight

into Lana from reception, dressed in a shroud from the mortuary, her face painted like a skull.

He fainted.

Shelly Curtis was looking at Salinger. 'Sorry, Jim. But Happy New Century anyway!'

Mrs Trattorio hugged her purring cat a little tighter.

'Happy New Century,' she said, kissing its head.

The cat looked up and licked her hand.

Everyone at the Institute was partying wildly. Professor Wagg stared mournfully up at his failed clock, and then back at his guests.

He saw his beautiful daughter, Sophie, dancing with that young man she'd been with earlier. Gareth something, she had said. She was leaning forward and kissing him.

Professor Wagg was going to frown, then shrugged. 'Girls will be girls,' he muttered. He looked again at his clock, and then at his wrist watch.

'Oh, what the hell,' he said. 'Twenty. Nineteen. Eighteen . . .'

The other party-goers took up the chant.

'Seventeen. Sixteen.'

Sophie and her young man parted, both grinning from ear to ear.

'Fifteen. Fourteen.'

Champagne corks popped, people yelled and pumped hooters.

'Thirteen. Twelve.'

All across San Francisco, cars in the streets slammed on their horns in a huge cacophony of celebration.

Officer Buffini finished marking out her chalk figure of where Miranda Gerhardt had been found.

She looked over to Officer Selby. 'How long?'

Selby grinned and pointed to his watch.

'Eleven. Ten.'

Shelly Curtis was hugging Ted, Angela Wheeler and Jim Salinger.

'Group hug!' she shouted and loads of other guests moved towards them, making a huge ball of people in the centre of the room, all shouting.

'Nine. Eight. Seven.'

'Happy New Century,' yelled Salinger. 'It's gonna be great!'

'Six. Five. Four. Three. Two. One. Midnight!'

Balloons fell from the ceiling and everybody screamed, whooped and yelled delightedly as they moved into the new millennium.

★ ★ ★

The TARDIS materialised in the park.

The door opened, spilling bright light into the dark night, and three people hurried out, just in time to see the fireworks erupt all over the sky as midnight struck.

From over the water and from the city, voices could be heard, singing '*Should auld acquaintance be forgot . . .*'

'I never liked that song,' Grace said.

'Oh, I don't know,' said the Doctor. 'I've always had a soft spot for all things Scottish.' He pulled his straw hat out from under his coat, twirling it on his finger. '"Should auld acquaintance" indeed,' he murmured.

Chang Lee held out his hand. In it was the Doctor's fob-watch. With a broad grin, the Time Lord took it back. 'Thank you,' he said, clipping the chain on to his vest, and dropping the watch-face into the pocket. 'I was missing that.'

'Oh, and this, too.' The boy passed over the bag of gold dust.

The Doctor reached out and closed Chang Lee's hand around the bag. 'Keep it. Look after yourself with it. Oh, and next Christmas, take a good vacation. Just don't be here.'

Grace sighed. 'There you go, interfering again.'

The Doctor laughed. 'Well, Grace, now that you mention it, you ought not to –'

'Don't,' she said firmly.

'Why not?'

'Because I know who I am. That's enough.'

Chang Lee was staring at the gold in his hand, shocked. 'Are you sure, Doctor? I mean, I tried to – well, you know, the Master and I –'

The Doctor nodded. 'Yes, but that's in the past. Just make good use of your future.'

The boy grinned. 'Okay. I'm getting out of here before you change your mind.' He started walking backwards. 'See you around, Doctor. Dr Holloway.'

'Bye, Chang Lee.'

They watched as he ran across the park until he had been swallowed up by the trees and darkness.

'I'd better be off, too.' The Doctor half turned towards the TARDIS.

'Do you want to come with me?'

Grace pointed back downtown. 'Do *you* want to come with *me*?'

The Doctor glanced at the TARDIS, back towards the city and then at Grace. 'I'm tempted . . .'

Grace nodded. 'I guess you are. So am I.'

She reached forward and hugged him. One last time. Feeling his heart – hearts – beating, feeling his hands on her, hearing him breathing. She looked into his eyes. Clear, blue, powerful eyes. Strong eyes, no longer afraid.

'I'll miss you,' she said simply.

'Not me,' he said. 'I'm the guy with two hearts. I'm easy to find.'

'I didn't mean that –'

He put a finger to his lips. 'I know.'

She reached forward and kissed him.

'Thank you, Doctor,' she said quietly.

The Doctor straightened his cravat, and ran a hand through his hair. He passed his old straw hat over to her. 'And thank you. Doctor!'

Grace Holloway watched as the Doctor walked back into the TARDIS and closed the door behind him. She smiled as, with that strange trumpeting sound, the TARDIS faded away, taking the Time Lord out of her life as bizarrely and unexpectedly as he'd entered it.

Turning back towards civilisation, she popped the hat on her head, and wondered which party to head for.

Inside the console room, the Doctor punched some buttons and set the coordinates.

'Well, old girl, I don't know where I've just selected, but let's hope it takes us somewhere interesting, unusual and exciting.'

He patted the console. 'Or at least, somewhere that does a decent pot of tea.'

Also available from BBC Books:

The official script of the film
Matthew Jacobs

Read the complete script of the long-awaited new Doctor Who film, a co-production between BBC Worldwide and Universal Television. Starring Paul McGann as the Doctor, Eric Roberts as the Master and Daphne Ashbrook as Grace. With an introduction by Philip Segal, Executive Producer and featuring eight pages of colour photographs.

Available from all good bookshops.

ISBN 0 563 40499 X
Priced £5.99